© Timothy Allen

EDWARD ST. AUBYN lives in London with his two children. He is the author of *The Complete Patrick Melrose Novels* (*Never Mind, Bad News, Some Hope, Mothers Milk*, and *At Last*). *Mother's Milk* was short-listed for the Man Booker Prize in 2006. His novel *On the Edge* was published in the United States for the first time by Picador in 2014. His latest novel is *Lost for Words*.

"The Melrose novels are among the smartest and most beautiful fictional achievements of the past twenty years."

—*New York Observer*

"I read the five Patrick Melrose novels in five days. When I finished, I read them again." —Ann Patchett, *The Guardian* (London)

"Take P. G. Wodehouse's lighthearted country-house tales of the British aristocracy, then dip them in an acid bath of irony, drug abuse, and general decay, and you have Edward St. Aubyn's Patrick Melrose novels. . . . St. Aubyn's novels fall into that rare category of books that have been highly praised yet are still somehow underrated." —Scott Stossel, editor of *The Atlantic* (The Best Book I Read This Year)

"Highly entertaining and often devastatingly dark . . . The Melrose novels are modern masterworks of social comedy."

—*Bookforum*

"Edward St. Aubyn is probably neck-and-neck with Alan Hollinghurst for the title of 'purest living English prose stylist.'"
—Garth Risk Hallberg, *The Millions* (Most Anticipated Books of the Year)

"Why did it take me so long to fall in love with the brilliant novels of Edward St. Aubyn?" —Bret Easton Ellis

"The Melrose novels are a masterwork for the twenty-first century, written by one of the great prose stylists in England."

—Alice Sebold, author of *The Lovely Bones*

A CLUE TO THE EXIT

A NOVEL

Edward St. Aubyn

PICADOR

FARRAR, STRAUS AND GIROUX

NEW YORK

A CLUE TO THE EXIT. Copyright © 2000 by Edward St. Aubyn. All rights reserved. Printed in the United States of America. For information, address Picador, 175 Fifth Avenue, New York, N.Y. 10010.

www.picadorusa.com
www.twitter.com/picadorusa • www.facebook.com/picadorusa
picadorbookroom.tumblr.com

Picador® is a U.S. registered trademark and is used by Farrar, Straus and Giroux under license from Pan Books Limited.

For book club information, please visit www.facebook.com/picadorbookclub or e-mail marketing@picadorusa.com.

Library of Congress Cataloging-in-Publication Data

St. Aubyn, Edward, 1960–
    A clue to the exit : a novel / Edward St. Aubyn.—First U.S. edition.
        p. cm.
    ISBN 978-1-250-04603-1 (trade paperback)
    ISBN 978-1-250-04604-8 (e-book)
    1. Authors—Fiction.   2. Women gamblers—Fiction.   3. Terminally ill—Fiction.
I. Title.
    PR6069.T134C58 2015
    823'.914—dc23

                                                                                            2015018598

Picador books may be purchased for educational, business, or promotional use. For information on bulk purchases, please contact the Macmillan Corporate and Premium Sales Department at 1-800-221-7945, extension 5442, or write to specialmarkets@macmillan.com.

Originally published in Great Britain by Chatto & Windus

First U.S. Edition: September 2015

10 9 8 7 6 5 4 3 2

For Janey

ACKNOWLEDGEMENTS

I want to thank Francis Wyndham whose subtlety, sympathy and rigour make him the reader every writer is looking for.

Clearly you *move still in the human maze—but I like to think of you there; may it be long before you find the clue to the exit.*

—HENRY JAMES TO HUGH WALPOLE,

14 AUGUST 1912

A CLUE TO
THE EXIT

1

I've started to drive more cautiously since I was told I only have six months to live. All the love I've ever felt seems to have waited for this narrowing funnel of time to be decanted more precisely into my flooding veins. Bankrupt, I cannot resist staring through jewellers' windows at those diamond chokers locked solid around black velvet necks.

I've often wondered whether to commit suicide. I assume I needn't go into the temptations, but in a self-service world where you have to fill your own petrol tank, assess your own taxes, and help yourself to self-help, the one thing you don't have to do for yourself is end your life. So why not luxuriate in that old-fashioned sense of service? Go on, do yourself a favour, you know you deserve it: let something else finish you off.

As I watch the dying leaves turn red in the valley, I shudder with admiration. The defiance of that incandescent decrepitude, spitting in the face of its executioner: that's what I want. The smoke, wobbling up in diffident communion with the sky, thrills me less. It soon dilates over the reddening fields and sinks back to the clotted earth.

Red ochre was the first decorative material. Even *Homo erectus*, barely upright and still nervous on safari, one and a half million years before the delivery of the first armoured Land Rover, loved to rub a little rouge into her bearded cheeks. The linguists tell us that after black and white the first stain of colour in every lexicon is red. Once light and dark have been distinguished what's fundamental is blood and fire. Looking at the leaves turn red in the valley simplifies my mind, a javelin flying past those tightly packed tubes of paint in which so many subtle frequencies of light have been trapped, and landing where there is only blood and fire.

My doctor, who is unable to cure anything at all, has nevertheless 'given' me six months to live. I have never been given six months before and I don't know how to thank him adequately. If I die one day sooner he'll be hearing from my lawyers. One day later and he'll be hearing from me. He peeped over the parapet of his half-moon specs and gave me an indulgent smile, his expensive black pen writhing epileptically on the prescription pad. Prozac.

'No point in getting depressed on top of everything else,' he said.

'On top of what else?' I asked.

Until the brain transplant has been perfected, the only thing worth getting from a doctor is morphine. As to nurses, don't let them anywhere near you or they'll hike up their striped skirts and jab the precious liquid into that interval of white thigh between their black stockings and their sensible knickers.

The happy pills – I don't begrudge their happiness, nor do I envy it – are unopened on the shelf. I don't want any pills, shots, consoling books, or chats with chaplains. I just want to see if I can stay exactly where I am. This is after all the heart of the matter, the place where everything – not without difficulty, not without civil war, not without nailing down my tongue and drawing over it the serrated knife of one thing after another, not without learning to thank my torturers because it's been such a growth opportunity for all of us, not without betrayal always cutting its prices to meet the competition of feeling betrayed, not without the drive-by shootings of the desire for things which, let's face it, aren't going to happen, not without finding myself in the safety-deposit vaults with the unpinned grenade of involuntary memory, not without all the people I've hurt, been hurt by, and been hurt by being, scattering like cats' paws across an ocean of interstellar darkness, not without knowing that the things I mean most will be considered the most pretentious – this is still the place where everything might be reconciled. Reconciled by what? By the intolerable proximity of contradictions, by meltdown, by taking up residence in the Chernobyl of intimacy.

How convenient to frame that last paragraph with the revelation that it was written by a character we can all agree to find deranged. And yet how inconvenient to become the manager of yet another surrogate self, carrier of some cherished or despised qualities, vehicle for a certain story which demands to be shaped before it is blurted out. No, this time it's the first-person singular, the skydiver who forgot his parachute, the idiot who tries to tell it how it is; no Ted, Carol, Bob, or Alice, but the unadorned 'I', the pockmarked column standing alone among the ruins. It is midday and the shadow is briefly beneath its broken foot. It is 'I' and, yes, you've guessed it, milk-fed on manuals of rhetoric and seminal deconstructions of the art of writing, or perhaps reading a book for the very first time, it doesn't matter, you've still guessed it: 'I' is just as flimsy a fabrication as the rest of them, Ted, Carol, Bob, and Alice. So, what is the authentic ground of being, if this footling pronoun is so inessential?

2

I have to own up and admit that I've experimented with the Prozac. I know I said I wouldn't and I suppose that makes me an unreliable narrator, if that's what an unreliable narrator is.

What made me do it? It wasn't a sense of futility. I am consumed by the need to write something honest and complete before I die.

Fear, pure fear. Something's burning, something's on fire. It's me, I'm burning. Instead of standing quietly in the fireplace and agreeing to be a human log, I rush about setting fire to everything – tapestries, curtains, canvases – every one of them irreplaceable and none of them insured. It shows such a lack of consideration. Instead of my daughter being able to say, 'This is the house where we've lived since 1999,' ruins, just ruins. She might wrinkle up her nose and add, 'I mean, the point of that house was its things.' Whereas, if I showed a little consideration and left the Neo-Geo wheel and the Australian aboriginal rugs unscorched, she might say instead, with a strain of tenderness in her voice, 'Dad wasn't such a bad sort in the end.'

Well, it wasn't the fear either.

What made me take the Prozac was Lola. Lola is an unbelievably literary friend of mine and I've been dreading her call. What would I say to her gloating condolences? 'As you can imagine, I'm deep in Marcus Aurelius,' or, 'I find that these days I can only bear to listen to the very Late Quartets.' What would satisfy her greed for seriousness?

I hadn't had time to prepare anything when she sprang on me.

'Are you writing about it?'

'What?'

'Dying.'

'How did you find out?'

'Are you writing about it?'

'No. I don't think it's that interesting.'

'An opportunity missed. You know I've always thought you could do something serious.'

'It's wasted on me,' I said. 'It's all yours if you want it; no need to feel you're poaching on my territory.'

'Well, if I were dying . . .' she said. 'I remember you when you were an undergraduate – you were so interested in how the mind works. We expected great things of you and then you got sucked into that silly film world. Aren't you having any big thoughts at the moment?'

'Only big thoughts and very small ones. It's the medium-sized thoughts that jump ship in an emergency.'

'Write that down.'

'No,' I snapped, ending the call.

In any case, it's a good thing I'm taking the Prozac. I'm enjoying my positive attitude. It's got me making plans, being practical. The medium-sized thoughts are back. I may only have six months to live but I've still got to survive. I'm going to New York to see my agent, Arnie Cornfield. Arnie is famous for his introductory rap, 'Some people want an agent to hold their hand. Some people want a shoulder to cry on. Well, I'm not that kind of an agent. I'm interested in one thing and one thing only: money.'

When I was writing *Aliens with a Human Heart* (perhaps you were one of the fifty-three million people who paid to see it) I enjoyed pointing out to novelists struggling with a £3,800 advance spread over seventeen years that the novel is dead. Now that I'm about to join it I'm not so sure. Why should the novel die? Why should anybody die?

Arnie won't be pleased that I want to write a novel. Too bad. I just need enough money to see me out. This house I bought near St Tropez is expensive to keep up.

It's a pink house with white gates. At the front there are two palm trees, floodlit, so the burglars don't fall flat on their faces. At the back, four minuscule cypresses, like self-conscious bridesmaids, accompany the concrete driveway to the garage. If you climb on the roof and jump, you can see the sea. Inside there are still-empty niches everywhere, and tiny flights of steps leading from one thing to another. Two steps up to the kitchen, three down to the living area, one onto the patio, two into the garden, and a final glissando of steps back to the entrance area.

It's as if the builder had stumbled across the concept of a step and couldn't believe his luck. Get a load of this thing that goes up and down. *C'est un petit miracle.* Imagine the atmosphere of excitement on the building site, the dawning of a new possibility, like *Homo habilis* bringing a stone down for the first time on the bones of a scavenged gazelle and sucking out the marrow. The world would never be the same again.

The strange thing about these discoveries is that they often happen simultaneously in quite different places. It makes you think that ideas might be 'in the air'.

3

Is the oyster waiting for the lemon juice, or does the juice just fall? Who thought of bringing together elements from such remote worlds: oysters and lemons, ducks and oranges? It was you, you greedy thing. And so isn't it natural, in our delirium, on the borders between waking and insomnia, that we should imagine our death as the culinary triumph of a careless superior being? The bitter white splash of some unsuspected fruit, the stubby prongs, the big swallow.

From the way he tucked into his lunch at Mi Casa Ti Casa, I can only assume that Arnie Cornfield was not afflicted by these reflections.

'Nobody wants to hear about death,' he said, loading a dripping cable of *spaghetti alle vongole* into his mouth. 'It's depressing. The audience have gotta leave the movie with a smile on their faces.'

'But it's my only subject: I live it, I breathe it, I eat death.'

'Eat death, eat shit,' said Arnie. 'Gimme that feel-good factor, like you did in *Aliens with a Human Heart*.' His face lit up again. 'That was a beautiful deal.'

'But I'm not in that space any more,' I said. 'I've had some very serious medical news; as you will, if you live long enough. I've got to communicate what's happening – I mean,' I suddenly saw my opportunity, 'talk about "Wake up and smell the flowers".'

'*Smell the Flowers*, I like,' said Arnie. '*Smell the Flowers*, there's a market for. How about they get the files mixed up and he's not really dying at all – it's some other schmuck, a weirdo serial killer: someone who deserves to die.'

'But they didn't get the files mixed up, Arnie, this is happening to me. Don't you get it? I'm dying.'

'Who's your executor?' said Arnie. 'It's a dog-eat-dog world.'

'When did you last see a dog eat a dog?'

'Gimme a break, it's an expression, like . . . eh, "The pursuit of happiness" it's not meant to be taken literally, right?' Arnie wiped some of the orange sauce from his chin. 'Even after you die you gotta have representation, otherwise you're yesterday's news, *kaput, finito*.'

'Will you be my executor?' I simpered.

'I'd be honoured,' said Arnie. 'Tony!'

Tony came over. He's big in the theatre.

'You know Charlie.'

Tony smiled.

'We're planning a big retrospective of Charlie's work. *Boy Meets Girl, The Frog Prince* and, of course, the jewel in the crown, *Aliens with a Human Heart*. In about . . . how long is it, Charlie?'

'Six months.'

'Six months,' said Arnie.

'Congratulations,' said Tony.

I looked suitably modest.

'By the way, I've had a peep at your friend's manuscript,' said Tony, 'and I think what he's doing is very dangerous. One little rule we have in the theatre is *never* let the public into rehearsals. I don't know what's wrong with writers these days. I mean, why can't he just establish some credible characters . . .'

Arnie started nodding his head vigorously. 'Tell the fucking story.'

'And by imagining their lives,' Tony went on, 'explore the themes he wants to bring to our attention.'

'In other words, tell the fucking story,' said Arnie. 'Thanks for having a look at it, Tony. That's what I figured, but this guy comes highly recommended, and sometimes I think maybe I'm outta touch. I see so much material, I think maybe there's a market for this shit.'

Tony had to rush.

'What are ya gonna call it?' asked Arnie.

'*Smell the Flowers*,' I suggested.

'Sounds great. Send me the treatment and I'll get you the deal.'

4

It's midnight. I am in the Westbury Hotel, sweating over the outline for *Smell the Flowers*. Arnie doesn't even know that I want to write a novel yet, let alone the extent to which it will not be centred on a floral tribute. You would have thought that I could write a phoney outline for *Smell the Flowers* and then write the morbid novel I really have in mind, but I've made the fatal mistake of drawing a *cordon sanitaire* of honesty around the subject of my death.

Earlier today I started writing something a little magical. 'Magical, there's a market for,' as Arnie might say. News travels slowly from Paris to Bogotá, but from that ingenious capital it has pulsed around the world at the speed of light.

Doña S was always very particular about attending confession, no easy matter given that she was permanently asleep

and lived at the bottom of a well. The Jesuits from the semi-nary at San Sebastián refused to come over the mountains to our lonely little village, and so we chose my grandmother's donkey to be our priest. To us simple folk, Eeh-Aw might as well have been the Pope. Once a week at noon we would fol-low our beloved confessor to the well in a candle-lit procession, give him a bucket of carrots and leave him to listen to Doña S's seemingly chaotic but highly symbolical ramblings . . .

Charming as it might be to skip along in the Andean style, I've decided that whimsy is not the royal road to freedom, and that I have to return to the one fact I can rely on: that I, who-ever I am, am dying.

The trouble is that when the mind is fixed on dying everything starts to spiral and to magnify. Have you noticed how many spirals there are? Double helixes, spiral galaxies, cork-screws. They are hints of the mental habits that dying brings. Maybe if I settle into the helter-skelter of my final thoughts, the sharp edges will start to curve, the oppositions start to flow into each other. I must let it happen, I must soften my gaze. Being sharp is just one thing. Why get hung up on it?

Imagine a very old, very lonely woman whose only wish is that somebody should really mind about her death. And then imagine her very reluctantly realizing that she's going to have to go it alone on this one too. Join her for a moment. It doesn't matter who she is.

That idea didn't take either. Instead, at five-thirty this morn-ing as the garbage trucks outside my window were grinding the detritus of Madison Avenue in their savage jaws, I wrote the following fragment.

Patrick climbed on board the two-forty-five for London Paddington. The pedantic emphasis on Paddington struck him as a rather shrill assertion of straightforwardness in a word-world grown too playful for its own good, as if the train might otherwise be hijacked by Doña S and, despite setting out from Oxford, dive under the metropolis and approach it from the east, terminating inconveniently at Liverpool Street station.

Patrick flicked past the notes he had taken at the consciousness conference, until he reached some more personal reflections recorded at the back of his notebook.

'Like St Francis I am wedded to poverty, but in my case the marriage has not been a success.'

It was not true. He had enough money to be getting on with.

'The night is young. I must try not to envy her too much.'

His own youth had been a nightmare from which he was grateful to be distanced.

He was exasperated by his craven need for elegance, disgusted by his own stylistic habits. Was it too late to change?

He only had six months to find out. Cirrhosis, of course. The reprimand of those young nights.

The truth was that he was desperate about everything and he would have to abandon his taste for aphorisms if he was going to get close to describing his feelings. Even the routine unhappiness of the strangers on the station platform devastated him. The feeling raged through him, like a burning rope he couldn't hold on to, although someone he loved was falling at the other end of it; it ripped the skin from his hands. As he walked down the platform he had felt the pressure to drag bits of dead language over himself, like cardboard blankets on a freezing night. But he remained utterly exposed.

I was too tired to go on, but before I fell asleep I felt the relief of writing a third-person narrative. It is so much more personal than a first-person narrative, which reveals too flagrantly the imposture of the personality it depends on.

As I lay on the bed, spiralling into sleep, I realized that I couldn't grab at anything any more. I couldn't even grasp the simplest idea. Nothing would take hold. The chains of cause and effect were heaped uselessly at my feet. Maybe that's what freedom is like, only less drowsy.

5

Yesterday I doubled the dose of Prozac and despite my unhappy situation I feel quite violently cheerful. My mind is busy, busy, busy. I just don't see how I'm going to fit dying into my packed schedule. In December I'll be writing a deathless work of art. January's no good, I'm having a reconciliation with my ex-wife. The spring's out – it's the cherry season, for God's sake. The summer's not looking good either: my daughter is coming down to the coast to say a last farewell; I wouldn't miss that scene for all the world. We're going to have to reschedule this thing for next autumn. I know it's a whole year, but what can I do? I'm sorry.

Busy, busy, busy.

This morning I realized that my true subject – at least, for the purpose of getting an advance – is not death, but consciousness. It was Patrick going to that conference that gave me the hint. I rang Arnie's secretary and made an appointment for the next day, then I went to Brentano's and bought all the books on consciousness I could lay my hands on.

Luckily, I've done a speed-reading course and by the time I arrived at Mi Casa Ti Casa I had been able to scan twenty-six books with the word 'mind' in the title, as well as a rogue volume called *Now and Zen*. Unluckily, I am only able to retain for a few hours an impression of the material I read at this punishing pace, and the first dozen books had already faded on the drive over. Still, I was unlikely to forget the central point: nobody has a clue how consciousness works. That's why it's such a fertile field for fiction, unlike the steam engine, for instance, which is relatively well understood.

I found Arnie ripping the shell off a lobster and pouring a little battered tin of melted butter over its quivering body.

'This is better than sex,' he commented. 'You got that treatment for me?'

'I'm not writing about death any more.'

'You're just like my wife,' he said, and chuckled. 'She goes to the doctor every day. It's an illness: hypochondria. She thinks she's dying. I have to work my ass off so she can afford to be hysterical. So what's the new project?' he asked, expertly lowering the entire lobster down his throat like a sword-swallower.

'It's a novel,' I said.

Although he had a claw sticking out of each corner of his mouth, Arnie's indignation allowed him no pause.

'An ovel!' The claws appeared to become animated as he mumbled. 'What the fuck you writing an ovel fo? Ovelist is the schmuck gets aid peanuts for the wights if, ig if, he finds a poducer.'

'It's about consciousness,' I persisted.

Arnie spat out the claws. They clattered onto the plate, the flesh sucked from their shattered exoskeletons.

'What's the story line?' he mocked. 'Consciousness meets consciousness, they become super-conscious and live consciously ever after?'

'You must be psychic,' I said.

'Sure I'm psychic,' said Arnie, reluctant to refuse a compliment. 'Listen, Charlie, first you tell me you can't get death off your mind; now you tell me you can't get your mind off your mind. Sounds like you oughta sack your therapist and write a sequel to *Aliens with a Human Heart*. Don't you have any sense of social responsibility? Fifty-three million people are waiting for that sequel. Now, Charlie,' said Arnie, all avuncular, 'I know consciousness is a hot topic on the campuses. Did you read *Mind Matters*?'

'I must have done,' I said, feeling the memory of another dozen books slide down Lethe's greasy banks.

'How about *Mind Your Language*?'

'I . . . I think so.'

'That was a nice deal. The man who represented that book is a personal friend of mine. You wouldn't believe what some of these academic boys get paid. But a novel, Charlie, a novel. You gonna put synapses in a novel?'

'I don't have to put them in, they're in there already. My synapses are totally committed to this project,' I gushed. 'That's the beautiful thing about it, talk about "the medium is the message", this is the big one. Medium—message, form—content, they just kind of make out with each other the whole time.'

'You're writing a pornographic novel about consciousness?'

'I could,' I said obligingly. 'I was going to set it at a conference.'

'All they ever do at conferences is screw, right?' said Arnie, chucking back a double espresso.

'Lecture and screw.'

'Drop the lectures; just go right into the passion,' he advised.

'They could have thoughts about the lectures while they were screwing and thoughts about the screwing during the lectures. It would be a metaphor for the total interpenetration . . .'

'Total interpenetration, there's a market for,' said Arnie with a wink.

By now I was floundering. All I could remember from my reading was a couple of lines from *Now and Zen*.

'Listen to the wind moving through the pines,' I stammered.

'What fuckin' pines? This is Third Avenue. You having a psychotic episode? You think you're in the Pokanos?'

'The sound of the traffic, then,' I said. 'It doesn't matter.'

'What d'ya mean, it doesn't matter? You have any idea how much it costs to rent in this neighbourhood?'

'In the sound of the wind moving through the traffic is all the teaching we'll ever need . . .'

'Right,' said Arnie, cocking his ear towards the door. 'It's telling me I'm late for a meeting.' He heaved himself up from the table and left with a marked lack of ceremony.

I think I blew the pitch.

6

I'm back in St Tropez. Arnie is right: there's no real market for death or consciousness. I'm going to have to go it alone on this one. I've taken a last handful of Prozac and thrown away the bottle. My whole New York trip was a Prozac mirage. Thank God I didn't get the deal; this way I'm free, free as the wind, the open road. I'm going to get rid of this house and spend the last few months of my life in a hotel.

The estate agent who sold me the house for four million francs, a Welsh windbag with bright orange hair called Dai Varey, says that if I put it on the market for three million he can get rid of it 'in a jiffy'. He arrived wearing a blue blazer with heraldic buttons and a humorous tie with pink elephants trunk-to-tail from neck to navel.

'What I tell my clients,' he said, 'is forget the Alpes Maritimes and come to the Var. The air's like champagne, the sea's as clean as a whistle, and the natives are friendly.'

'I remember,' I said.

We walked to the end of the terrace and looked at the small valley in front of the house, still agricultural, like a streak of cortisone in the psoriasis of development.

'That's breathtaking,' said Dai. 'Those red leaves are an absolute knockout. May I ask, if it's not too personal a question, why you're leaving in such a hurry?'

'I'm dying.'

'Oh dear, I'm sorry to hear that,' said Dai, relieved. 'It comes to all of us in the end, doesn't it? Only, I had a very nasty experience with a *molto presto* sale that fell through because the vendor turned out to be involved in activities which were of more than casual interest to the boys in blue, if you know what I mean. You can imagine how interested the gendarmerie were in my commission. Fortunes of war, eh, fortunes of war.'

True to his word, Dai got rid of the house in a jiffy and sold it later that afternoon.

'That was quick,' I said.

'I bought it myself,' he explained, standing on the chimney stack and admiring the sea view. 'It seemed such a bargain. I couldn't believe my luck, a house like this coming on to the market at three million francs.'

Why would I regret leaving this sanctuary, with its Vietnam-movie soundtrack of choppers overhead, gunfire from the scrap of woodland that's left standing, the drone of a low private plane, the whistle of a higher jet, the chain-saw whine of the circling motorcycles, and the frantic honking of adulterous wives racing home through crowded lanes?

One of the great things about dying is that if you liquidate all your assets you can really pump up your monthly income. With half a million francs a month, I can move into the Hôtel du Grand Large in Villefranche-sur-Mer. My daughter will be all right; her mother kept our house in Belsize Park, although she says that her 'real home' is Tibet.

As I was leaving the house for the last time, the phone rang. It was my ex-wife, Heidi.

'I was just thinking about you,' I said.

'So what?' she said. 'How many times have you thought about me without getting a call?'

'Thousands,' I said, admitting the justice of her argument.

'Is that all, you stingy bastard?'

'Let's not argue,' I pleaded. 'I've been told that I have only six months to live.'

'Don't forget that death is a crucial moment in your spiritual development,' she said.

'How is Ton Len?'

'Oh, she's so sweet at the moment. She's obsessed with levitation. You're missing her at her most adorable.'

'I know,' I said.

'One day she'll realize that these fancy tricks are all very well for impressing simple people at country fairs, but they are nothing compared to the joy and compassion that spring from the realization of emptiness.'

'Naturally,' I said. Heidi gets very touchy if I question her grasp of Tibetan culture, and so I just agree to everything. 'Any chance of seeing her?' I asked, opening the old wound.

'None at all,' she said.

'I'm going to be dead soon.'

'All the more reason not to get her overexcited. It's typically selfish of you trying to get your child attached to something so ephemeral.'

'I just want her to know that I love her,' I said, beginning to cry.

'Was it very loving to fuck that chambermaid when you thought I was out skating with Ton Len? Was it very loving to cut me out of a co-producer's credit on the *Aliens* deal? Was it . . .'

I put the phone down on a cushion and went outside. I knew the speech off by heart and knew that I had between six and seven minutes to sob uncontrollably in the garden.

When I picked up the phone again, Heidi was saying, 'I sometimes wonder if you listen to a word I say.'

'I thought you were committed to loving-kindness,' I said wearily.

'I *am*,' she protested. 'Except when I hate somebody. Like all Tibetan-styled people I'm basically happy and giggly. If you get reborn as something cuddly and snugly, we might adopt you. A bouncy puppy,' she suggested, 'or a little kitty cat. There are monks who can follow you into the Bardo consciousness and out the other side. It's awesome. You wouldn't believe what some of these guys can do. It's so cool being Tibetan.'

'Far out,' I said. 'But no chance in this lifetime.'

'None at all,' said Heidi. '*Ciao*, baby. See you round the universe.'

7

Sometimes when I arrive in a hotel room I feel free, and then I remember what I'm free from, and I slide down the wall, staring at the mini-bar. After that, I like to get my bearings, check out the public rooms, scout for places to write.

Walking through the garden, testing the benches and the views, I saw a figure familiar to movie-lovers the world over. He walked pensively along the gravel path, in shoes thinner than tightropes, flanked by two top models dressed in nurses' uniforms.

'Charlie,' he drawled in his fabulous Italian accent, 'it's good to see you, my friend.'

'Maestro,' I said, kissing his hand.

'No, no, please,' he said, aspiring to embarrassment.

'How are you, Maestro?' I asked.

'At the moment I feel very flat,' he said.

The way he said 'flat' opened up vistas of choking richness, indomitable classicism and mischievous wit.

'In the Sixties,' he said, walking over to the railings at the edge of the sea, 'there arose around Godard a group of directors who asked the question, "*Qu'est-ce que c'est le cinéma?*' Now that the world is flooded with audiovisual imagery, I do not think that this question can be asked any more.' Unimpeded by the sable overcoat that dangled from his shoulders, he spread his hands despairingly, as if to offer the Mediterranean as evidence of this cluttering deluge. 'I have always been half inspired by cinema and half by life, but the young people today don't know anything about the history of cinema. If I make allusions, they don't pick them up.'

'But, Maestro,' I said, 'there's still room for passion and intelligence. You of all people—'

'There is passion and intelligence,' he interrupted, 'but there is no language for expressing them.'

'English,' I suggested.

He laughed. 'Charlie, I always liked your sense of humour. You are still young,' he said, clasping my arm: 'find that language, express that passion.' He started to cough violently. 'Excuse me,' he sighed. The two nurses, frowning at me significantly, guided him back indoors.

I stood alone for a long time, as if touched by destiny. I had been given my instructions by the Maestro: 'find that language, express that passion.' What perfect timing. I was alone in a hotel, where nobody knew how to get hold of me, and I could feel that last handful of Prozac evacuating my depressed body, like children in the Blitz. There was nothing to stop me writing until I dropped.

That evening in the dining room, with its panels of Zuber wallpaper disclosing a tropical landscape, as I sipped the best *potage de légumes jardinières* I have ever tasted, I felt myself slide into a more lugubrious rhythm. I started to write a note about the continuation of *On the Train*, when I was interrupted by a lively old countess with blue-rinse hair and wrinkles as fine as anything in a Holbein portrait. When she found out that I was a writer, she asked me if I used a pen or one of these new computers she had read so much about.

I told her that I cut open my wrist and collected the blood in my cupped hand and, using a six-inch nail, scratched out my sanguine words on the hides of snow leopards.

That shut her up.

8

This morning a funeral hearse arrived at the back of the hotel.

'*Madame la comtesse est morte*,' explained the concierge, drawing the side of his hand slowly across his throat and letting his tongue hang out, in case I didn't understand French.

I was overwhelmed with guilt. Why had I been so unfriendly to that vivacious old blue-rinse? Now she was dead and it was no use offering her a Kir royale before lunch. It's not enough to live each day as if it's your last, unless you remember that it's everybody else's last day as well. The grief a loving son would feel, and of which I had no inkling when my own mother was lowered into her flinty grave, tornadoed through me at the news of the countess's death.

'All one can do is set an example,' my mother used to say.

'Or make an example of someone else,' my father would add.

And it was all they could do.

Sometimes wild ideas were in the air. 'People did things with tremendous style in those days,' my mother occasionally re-marked, but it turned out that these stylish people simply trav-elled with an unusual amount of luggage, or had allowed themselves to take a favourite terrier on a military campaign, and that, in any case, 'those days' were hopelessly remote from life in our Tudor farmhouse in Staffordshire.

I once dared to complain that I had been brought close to breakdown by my parents' exemplary deadness.

'You seem to have turned out perfectly all right,' said my mother tranquilly.

'Perfectly all right,' said my father, in a tone which suggested that 'all right' was all wrong.

As I wept in the garden of the hotel, I realized that I was not crying for the countess or for my mother, but with frustra-tion at not having had a mother who deserved my tears. I dread the prospect of the pressure of death roaming through my psy-che like a wildcat prospector and producing these eruptions of unwelcome insight. I wish my mother had been right when she accused me of not wanting to 'make a contribution'. It would be so lovely to be good at doing nothing, but nothing is the one thing I cannot do.

Later, I saw the Maestro leave for Rome in a black Lambor-ghini. I couldn't help noticing that his chauffeur was dressed as one of the charioteers in *Ben Hur*. There's nobody quite like the Maestro. My helplessness prevented me from saying goodbye, but his departure added to the determination of my melancholy.

Feeling too upset to write, I made the brave decision to write about feeling too upset. At that precise moment when I was majestically uncapping my pen, a strikingly beautiful woman walked into the bar, where, despite my liver condition, I had just finished my seventh espresso.

Her hazel eyes threw out sparks of green fire from behind the loose spirals of her golden-brown hair. We looked at each other with unassailable hunger, knowing that sex would only usher us into an Ethiopia of desire where we would taste even more keenly the tragic knowledge that true intimacy cannot be shared.

Who ever allowed a little thing like that to interfere with a fuck?

On the contrary, our tragic lucidity and, of course, the frantically life-affirming atmosphere of a recent death stimulated us to a savage interrogation of each other's bodies. She drew blood with her nails and sucked the wounds like the flavour from a water ice. I rolled my forehead against hers, trying to break through the fortress of our lonely skulls and meld our yearning minds. We thrashed like marlin caught on the hooks of each other's unforgiving genitals.

'It's incredible how I can feel you in my cunt,' she said. 'I can feel your passion and your intelligence.'

At least I think that's what she said. French is not a language I claim to understand perfectly. For all I know she was saying, 'For God's sake get off me, I've got to get home and make dinner for my husband.'

And so the Maestro has left, without leaving behind any more detailed instructions to shape my destiny. The countess is dead, depriving me of one of those rich friendships that two people, no longer in perfect health, strike up in a luxury hotel. An opportunity to look back on two lives and decide that, on balance, they were very much worth living: all that's gone down the drain. And I've had sex with a stranger. I'm burning through my options fast. Soon there'll be nothing left to do but write.

9

This morning I am certain that the last traces of Prozac have been exiled by my imperious sadness. Why not get some more? Why not be a little lenient? Why not go and play blackjack in Monte Carlo, or visit Luxor? Why not invite a friend to share my five-star decline?

I drive myself to the edge because it is where I already am, stranded on a narrow atoll between what is not worth saying and what cannot be said, dead language and lost love on one side, silence and death on the other. The people I love are already out of reach, guarded by a jealous mother, or married to somebody else. And my friends would only try to console me. As to death, the only thing everyone manages to agree on is that this particular body, through which I have registered everything I know, whether it was hard-wired or acquired, generated or received, by chance or by design, freely or not, this particular body will end. Even fans of the near-death experience need a central nervous system to experience their disembodiment. Whatever death brings, it will not be the *potage de légumes jardinières* I enjoyed on Monday night, or yesterday's astonishing carnal adventure. Whatever may be left will be alien to the person I am now, and so only the part of me that is acquainted with strangeness will not be distracted by death. When he was dying, Molière asked for red wine and ripe cheese; Aldous Huxley, on the other hand, asked for mescaline. One can't be too careful in such an extreme situation, and I intend to have a slap-up dinner followed by a strong dose of mescaline.

In the meantime, I will continue *On the Train*. I want to know what's been going on all these years. I've thought that I was having consciousness and now it turns out I don't know what that means. I think I'll just introduce a new character. There's no time for bridge passages with a five-month deadline.

Crystal sat down opposite Patrick. She still found it difficult to lower herself into a chair without wincing, and her neck brace made her feel like a collared ox dragging a plough through a paddy field. She had been told more than once that after a car accident like that she was lucky to be alive. Her transcendentally beautiful near-death experience – or NDE, as the members of her new club called it – made it even harder for her to hear this earnest platitude. Peter was still in a coma, and the drunken diplomat who had run into them by the simple device of driving on the wrong side of the road was using the moral vaccine of diplomatic immunity.

Crystal would not have forced her shattered body to

Oxford for any other conference, but caught between the ethics
of switching off Peter's life support, the troubling status of
her NDE, and the rage she still felt towards the diplomat, she
figured that a consciousness conference was 'just the ticket',
as Peter would have said.

Would she ever hear him say it again? Every detail of his
voice, his tendency to mumble, his English accent, his pauses
and sudden rushes, seemed more precious to her now that she
might never hear them again. She felt guilty about leaving
him for three days, but she rang the hospital between every
lecture. No change. She had spent the last four weeks in
Peter's hospital room, talking to him as if he might reply at
any moment, kissing his face, reading to him, meditating with
his hand in her lap, and drawing his profile, telling him he
was the best model she'd ever had.

Tracy, the prim English nurse who was sometimes on
duty, and who already disapproved of Crystal's constant presence in Peter's room, as if it was akin to necrophilia, found
her sketching his impassive face. She stood for a while next
to the bed, fiddling with the sheets.

'Do you think that's really fair?' she finally asked, with the
air of someone defending the handicapped from exploitation.

Crystal realized that Tracy saw Peter as a quasi-corpse
to whom a quasi-funereal respect was due, a proper silence,
a few flowers and some make-up. Crystal was defiantly but
also quite naturally treating Peter as if he was still there. She
was drawing Peter because he was still Peter, not sneaking
up on him now that he could no longer protest. She tried to
communicate all of this with her steady gaze, but Tracy

looked back at her with equally steady conviction that she knew kinky behaviour when she saw it.

All the fascinating speculative questions Crystal might have hoped to answer by attending the conference were subsidiary to this leading question, 'Is Tracy right?'

The conference was not designed to answer her particular preoccupation. It revelled in all kinds of fringe experiences: the *petit mal*, the Korsakov's syndrome, the neurological dysfunctions that Oliver Sacks had made into a middlebrow passion; the pets who knew their owners were coming home; the twins separated at birth and living in distant cities who purchased the same dress on the same day; the flight of homing pigeons; the astral journeys of psychotic patients; the minuscule but robust incidents of paranormal phenomena; the consciousness which civilization had gained and the consciousness it had lost. There were of course philosophers with their qualia and their Artificial Intelligence. And some doctors, mapping out brain function in a style no less convincing than medieval cartography.

I have to interrupt Crystal's story because something absolutely extraordinary has just happened.

I was sitting in a cafe called Le Nautique, writing *On the Train*, when a woman at the next table asked me for a light. There was a gentle breeze, so I bunched three matches together and struck them, cupping my hand around the end of her Marlboro. Only then did I look up and notice her face. Her teeth were the colour of burnt oranges, and her dark-rose lipstick described a pair of lips at some distance from the ones that sucked on her cigarette. The swollen bags under her eyes trembled and twitched, but the eyes themselves stared resolutely into mine.

'You are writing a novel,' she said, in that cultivated French which is always such a pleasure to listen to.

'Yes,' I admitted.

'You will have a great success with your novel, a worldwide success.'

'How do you know?' I asked, casual but far from indifferent.

'You've heard of Henri Arnaud?'

'No.'

'He was the greatest psychic in France and he gave me his gift. I also do psychic surgery,' she went on. 'I learnt it from Dr Fritz in Brazil.'

'The borders between different dimensions are more liquid there,' I said encouragingly.

'Yes,' she said, giving me a burnt-orange smile. 'I like Brazil.'

She was clearly a woman of many talents and I was hugely relieved by the news she gave me about my novel. I felt the deep sense of peace that came from knowing I was doing exactly the right thing with the little time I have left.

Tonight, I sat in the hotel restaurant and let everything fall away except that sense of peace. As I breathed in I could feel my consciousness expanding along a glistening spider's web of total connectedness and as I exhaled it accordioned back into the tropical richness of my body, the streams and rivers of my blood. My breath rode untroubled across the huge intellectual divide that separates the primacy of sensation from universal consciousness.

I sat amazed in front of the burnt-sugar aviary of my *myrtilles Metternich*. Night-blue fruit caged in starlight.

Everything was utterly perfect.

10

This morning, I feel desperate again. Yesterday's elation might as well have happened to an entirely different person. What depths of self-delusion could have made me believe that crazy old witch in Le Nautique?

I must get out of this hotel. Luxury is too superficial to touch the real causes of depression; it conjures up the mirage of consolation and adds the whiplash of betrayal to an already miserable situation. It may be that nomadic life is our natural condition and that possessions exhaust us. But reception desks exhaust us too. Of course I love hotels. They are a kind of alienated, postponed, provisional home that suits me perfectly. I hate them for the same reason. This hotel which charmed and liberated me for a few days now magnifies my agitation. A delivery truck has just made the windows of my bedroom shake. If the

slow liquid of the glass is shaking, isn't the quicker liquid of my
blood shaking too?

I have now moved down to the bar to continue writing this
note, but it's impossible to concentrate with the muted music
shimmering out of the speakers like pins and needles. Only an
orchestra of terrified mice could scratch out a tune at this volume, and yet I wouldn't want it any louder.

Should I move? Should I cultivate the nomad? It would be
such a waste of time, even if I stayed on this coast. There are grand
hotels all the way from Cannes to Italy, vanilla and strawberry
palaces in their *vastes parcs fleuris*, sheltered by parasol pines and
fountaining palm trees. What difference does it make which one
I'm in?

The more fundamental problem is the sinister equation
'time is money'. It held true when I was running out of both, but
since I sold my house I have an abundance of money and with it
an involuntary softening of my focus on the neck of the hourglass. I realize that the people who really belong in these hotels
– not the honeymooners or the desperadoes like me, but people
like that woman in the corner who has smoothed her lizard skin
with surgery and the man next to her, his paunch guillotined by
the expert cut of his double-breasted suit – are really buying the
illusion of abundant time, meted out to them in canapés and
logoed bath robes and the swirling sea scum of 'Fingal's Cave'
currently being disgorged by the mouse orchestra.

I must cut through this illusion; I must restore myself to a
level of poverty commensurate with my medical condition. I
must get back to the heart of the matter: nothing being other
than it is, time utterly smooth, utterly innocent of any possible

alteration. Down there, I couldn't even choose the time of my death by committing suicide. It would just be another moment, utterly bald, innocent of all possible alteration. The horror of that and the bliss. The compacted contradictions. Meltdown.

The only way forward is to gamble. Tomorrow evening, when I've got the cash together, I will go to Monte Carlo with half my remaining funds, about 1.2 million francs, and throw them away on the roulette tables.

Now that I've made that decision, I have purchased enough calm to write. Even the strangled perkiness of this Mozart concerto cannot defeat me. I think I should put one more character on the train with Crystal and Patrick. I like to get my characters in one place at one time. The unities. I know it's old-fashioned, but consciousness is complex enough without characters moving around all over the place, except of course in imagination and memory.

Jean-Paul had always been fanatically curious about the nature of his own mind. At his primary school he'd been punished for hanging upside down from the fire escape, but when he told the headmaster that he'd been testing the effects of more blood flowing to the brain Monsieur Jourdan had privately predicted that Jean-Paul would become a great savant. By the age of eleven, he was eating a plate of Roquefort before going to bed, in the hope of adding to the splendour of his dreams. He had a torch and notebook under his pillow and a chewed ballpoint tied to a string around his wrist. Jolting out of his rank and troubled sleep he would transcribe his dream images before they slipped beneath the horizon of consciousness. As he grew older, he plunged into philosophy and psychoanalysis and emerged from the usual succession of *hautes* French schools as an advocate of Lacan and the other giant *intellos* of his youth.

Meeting Crystal had returned him to experiment and disobedience. The loss of self engendered by the psychedelic voyage she had taken him on in Utah's Canyonlands had been pivotal to his development. It destroyed his faith in the priority of linguistic structures. Of course generative grammar had a hard-wired, impersonal chic, it was the matrix for making sense, but it was neither what he experienced in conscious-ness nor did it seem to him the ground of being.

The egalitarian chaos of his psychedelic experience high-lighted the roles of empathy and analogy. At first he tried to contain this chaos: surely there were choices behind these analogies, desires behind the choices, psychological struc-tures behind the desires, and, underlying the psychology, the stainless steel of generative grammar. This analysis made him feel false, made him feel he was resisting an insight rather than having one. It was untrue to the quality of his experience, to the plasticity of his choices, the molten emer-gence and reabsorption of images. As he allowed the old order to be dismembered, a new erotic order arose in which there was an unceasing intercourse between sensation and conception, the mental blossoming of every sensation and the embodiment of every idea.

He concluded that only the tyranny of talk had made thought seem like an internal conversation. He was now re-luctantly drawn into a pre-linguistic realm where sensations gave rise to images and images to empathy and empathy to analogy, with words attaching themselves quite late in the process, if at all, like advertising executives promising to promote a product. The images sometimes naively took them on. And even those late-coming words could turn into sensations as easily as any other idea. If he said *'colombe'*, for instance, he had a spherical sensation, like a marble rolling quietly round the groove on the rim of a solitaire board. The English word 'crazy', on the other hand, ripped through him like shrapnel.

I must suspend the writing of *On the Train* for a moment in order to go to Monte Carlo and throw away half my remaining capital in the Salles des Jeux. I expect to be able to accelerate my production once I've reduced my income to a more uncomfortable level. It was rather a business getting hold of all that cash but I now have it in a small suitcase. I have to admit that I find the whole situation rather enthralling.

11

Gambling is wonderful. It breaks my heart that I've taken so long to discover it. On the other hand, ripeness is all, and there could be no more perfect moment to become addicted to this exhilarating new vice. It's all very well to cultivate pure Being, but in order to become a well-rounded person one must also cultivate pure Chance.

I had never been to the casino in Monte Carlo before. The passport formalities warned me that I was entering another country, with its own dialect, its own currency of lustrous plastic counters and, above all, its own sense of time, sealed off from natural light and measured in spins and deals. If time is money, I was entering an eternity where all its other aspects were carefully falsified. I was at the heart of the delusion which I could only escape by penetrating more deeply.

I explained my predicament: the inconvenience of walking

around all evening with a suitcase. The management obligingly took my suitcase and gave me two yellow and white chips with 500,000 written on them in large gold numbers, and two smaller green and white chips with 100,000 written on them in smaller gold numbers.

'That's better.' I smiled, admiring the snug way they fitted into the four pockets of my jacket.

A man with the understanding eyes of a confessor said apologetically that he hoped I could produce documentation for such a large sum of cash. I was unknown to the establishment and sometimes criminal elements tried to use the casino to launder their money. I explained that I was faced with the prospect of premature death and saw no reason not to liquidate my assets and gamble. He seemed entirely satisfied, not to say excited, by my situation. I spared him my literary ambitions; I didn't have all night to chat about the meaning of life.

Privately, I was obsessed with the logic of my decision. If I could cast off the heavy cloak of luxury, I would be able to write with that passionate concentration I need in order to say something true before I die. I would be embedded in the trickling sand of the hourglass. I would become as intimate with my own experience as a neck with a noose. I would strip my life down to a whitewashed room, a chair, a desk, a page, a pen. And the birth canal to this proud simplicity was the Salle d'Europe; cliffs of gold, azure shields, garlanded nymphs, and roulette tables, themselves arranged like the spokes of a wheel under the circular golden grid of the ceiling. I became so caught up in this paradox that I had to walk round the room again and again, trying to tune my mood to the great act of intensification I was about to perform.

As I circled the tables I started to notice that not only the *belle époque* decoration but the physiognomies of the staff and gamblers were devices for arresting time. There was a haughty tail-coated footman with white hair and a Roman nose. And a heavy-lidded corrupt waiter who gave available-for-flogging glances. There was a gambler with long curly hair and a muske-teer's zip of black beard in the cleft of his chin. He had a diamond earring, a yellow silk tie and a half-oriental girlfriend with white make-up and purple half-moons of exhaustion under each glit-tering black eye. There was a crowd of powder-caked, chain-smoking old women weighed down with jewellery. I saw an oriental man with a scar down the left side of his face and a bored tart in tow, smoking, chipless, on the stool next to him. He was also wearing a thick gold bracelet studded with diamonds. I saw jewellery everywhere, and realized that what looked like finan-cial confidence was in fact the sign of how little these gamblers trusted themselves with money. When they had nothing left in their pockets, at least they still had thousands of pounds squeezed around their fingers, wrists and necks.

I couldn't help noticing that most people were playing with twenty- and fifty-franc chips. There were some pink five hun-dreds and blue thousands, but I knew that my 100,000-franc block was bound to be noticed and so, shy as a virgin, when a virgin is shy, I walked over to an empty table where an idle crou-pier sat alone. I placed the green and white counter on the red diamond and looked at him pleadingly, hoping he would take it away before it attracted any curiosity. A couple of tourists drifting by immediately glued themselves to the table and watched the ivory ball bounce its way into a slot. My prayers were answered. It was black. I met their commiserating expressions with a smile of subtle satisfaction. One hundred thousand francs in under two minutes. What lightness. What clarity of purpose.

I resumed my pacing, hoping to ditch the spectators, and the moment they were on the other side of the room I returned to the empty table and quickly dropped a second counter on 'Manque'. I had no idea what it meant in casinoland, but its ordinary French meaning of 'lack' seemed fitted to my purpose, and indeed I was soon lacking a second 100,000 francs. The satisfaction that accompanied this second loss was tainted by a hollow feverishness, an accelerated pulse, a longing to repeat the act. I was displeased by this impurity. I wanted to taste freedom, not burden myself with some new set of suspect pleasures. I retreated to the casino restaurant, Le Train Bleu, in order to dispel this trace of confusion and prepare myself for an absolutely calm abandonment of my last million francs. I would have to go deeper into the bowels of the casino, to the Salle Privée, where my 500,000-franc counters would be in their natural habitat.

In the meantime, I sat in the fake train compartment of the restaurant, entombed in buttoned-leather padding. Beside me was a glass case filled with old tin toys, and a hand-written card saying: WE BUY OLD TIN TOYS. Here in the kingdom of old tin toys, it was all right to be an old tin toy oneself, or an old tin toy-boy for that matter. The grandest toy of all was a great big Italian gunboat. What bliss to be behind those portholes, in the ultimate sealed-off chamber, in the boat, in the case, in the train, in the casino, with great big guns to stop anyone interrupting you – doing what? – playing, of course. *Les jeux sont fait*, never mind the torpedo in the engine room.

The two women at the neighbouring table spoke in Russian. Hearing that sibilant and barbaric tongue undulating once more through the Salle d'Europe, I reflected on the opportunities for portraying the sickness of a continent through the gaping metaphor of a great casino: the confluence of nations, the teasing combination of formality and mental illness and, above all, the trick of chasing the whore of Fortune while ignoring the fact that time is running out. Naturally, I thought of Thomas Mann's cosmopolitan morbidity, Dostoevsky's compulsive gambling, and the Grand Duke Dmitri, exiled to the South of France for helping to murder Rasputin, and missing the excitement of the Russian roulette back home.

With only five months to live, I hardly had time to embark on such an ambitious narrative. I must content myself with carving the cherry stone of consciousness. And so I ordered a *risotto di aspergi e gamberoni*, which I can unhesitatingly recommend to anyone who is halfway through throwing their capital down the green-felt drains of Monte Carlo, and wrote the following fragment.

Perfect, thought Patrick, she's come to sit opposite me. He had seen her at the conference and was immediately drawn to this bruised and beautiful woman in a neck brace. Besides the sexual attraction, he felt an obscure but strong affinity with her, as if they were different aspects of the same intention. It

was hard to explain, but as she sat down opposite him, closing her eyes while she shifted into a tolerable position, he felt
the weight of his desperation become more widely distributed.
This was not a vague impression, it had the distinctness of a
broken table acquiring another leg.

Crystal smiled at him painfully. 'You were at the conference, right?'

'Yes.'

'Did you like it?'

'I liked this morning's Alzheimer doctor,' said Patrick.
'The one who said that if you treated the patient as if he were
there, "the whole manifestation changed".'

'Oh, yes, I liked him too,' said Crystal enthusiastically.
'You see, I've been treating Peter as if he was there. I ought
to explain that I had a car accident with my husband. I had
an NDE and he's still in a coma. We really should have been
hanging from the ceiling in a perspex cage during this conference, we've become such an ideal consciousness-studies
couple.'

'God,' said Patrick, 'I'm sorry to hear that.' He could tell
that this strain of humour was not quite natural to her.

'Oh, thank you. We were lucky to survive.' Crystal sighed.
'I have to say that, because I couldn't bear hearing someone
else saying it again.'

'It's not my kind of line,' said Patrick.

'Forgive me, but I wasn't going to take the risk. Yeah,'
she resumed, 'the Alzheimer doctor was good. That film interview was wonderful and terrifying at the same time. His
patient was losing the memory of language without losing

the sense of who he was. It suggests that the witness is more fundamental than the executive. When the one who acts collapses, there's still one to feel him collapse.'

'Absolutely,' said Patrick. 'And the people we treat as absent are in fact desperately frustrated, like a dream where you scream and nobody hears.'

'Except that you may not wake up,' said Crystal. 'In my NDE, I was in the operating theatre listening to the doctors talk about my poor prospects of survival and screaming at them to get the glass out of my neck. They just ignored me. So I try to listen to Peter.' Crystal's eyes filled with tears. 'Try to imagine what he might be wanting to say . . .'

Patrick could think of nothing to say. He smiled at Crystal, but she stared blindly through the windows of the train. Faced with the pressing prospect of premature death, Patrick felt that he could have been – that he would quite like to have been – in that perspex cage with Crystal, and if necessary the comatose Peter, dangling from the ceiling of the conference room.

He was reminded of Pierre, his old drug dealer from New York. The Ancient Mariner of Lower Manhattan, Pierre compulsively described his bizarre suffering to anyone who came within range. 'For eight fucking years I thought I was an egg, *je croyais que j'étais un oeuf*. But I had total consciousness, *une conscience totale*. I knew *everything*.' Unable to crack the ovular self-sufficiency of his body, his awareness left the hospital where he was being treated as a catatonic patient, and sped through a universe bathed in intelligence. From time to time he would return to the scene of his desertion and look down with a stranger's pity at the frozen body on the bed, at the nurses who came and went, carrying flannels and plates of food. But even Pierre, who was so fascinated by his ecstasy, refused to let go entirely of his body. Recognizing that it was dying of neglect, he forced himself back inside, squirming with reluctance, like a child who has to climb back into a wet bathing suit. 'I was totally disgusted, man. *J'avais un dégoût total.*'

Should Patrick tell Crystal the half-inspiring story of Pierre's return to animation? Pierre had been catatonic, Peter was in a coma, and neither of them had Alzheimer's. Still, there were analogies. If an Alzheimer's patient could go blank and yet know that he was going blank, and if the catatonic Pierre had total consciousness when he appeared to have none, who could confidently say that Peter had no idea what was happening to him?

As Patrick wondered how to revive his conversation with Crystal, a tap on the window drew his attention to a man waving at her from the platform. He recognized the Frenchman who had made a challengingly opaque presentation at the conference the day before.

I was forced to stop writing at this point. The waiter asked me for the fourth time whether there was anything more I wanted and I conceded a request for the bill. There was an atmosphere of insulation in that restaurant which Proust would have envied. A good casino is the perfect place to write: isolated without being lonely, single-minded and yet sophisticated, exclusive and welcoming at the same time; sealed off from the distractions of the world and sealed in a world of distraction, it has that oxymoronic tang that keeps one from falling asleep. I looked through the internal window of the restaurant at the gamblers drifting past like fish in an aquarium, drank the last of my coffee, closed my notebook, and plunged into the florid scene beyond the glass.

As I stepped into the Salle Privée, I immediately felt the uplift of its higher ceilings and the downpour of its weightier luxury. Two giant nymphs, representing Dawn and Dusk, reinforced the effort to arrest time by being interchangeable. Whether the sun rose or the sun set, nothing could interfere with their delicate self-absorption. Another night and several fortunes may have swirled down the plughole, and vast herds of human cells thrown themselves off the precipice of time, but nothing had really changed, because the evening's twin was there to greet the haunted gambler, still loitering in a rosy-fingered landscape, still dressed in the semi-diaphanous nymphwear she had borrowed from her sister the night before. Although I had to refuse their gentle invitation to pretend that time was not cutting my throat, I was delighted to be among people who had decided to come to their endless party so decoratively dressed.

Giving in to a childish ambition to get rid of one million francs in under five minutes, I asked one of the croupiers to place half a million on 14 – the date of my birthday – and then walked over to the neighbouring table to place my second half million on red. An individual number seemed absurdly unlikely to come up and I'd already had some luck losing on red. Returning to the first table, I heard an ominous murmur of astonishment and was appalled to find thirty-six half-million franc counters stacked up for me like building blocks in a children's game. Needless to say I was the centre of attention as I tried to stuff the unfortunate winnings into my pockets. I really needed a shopping bag, but I was too shy to ask. At the neighbouring table I found that red, at least, had not let me down, but the loss of one counter hardly made up for the burden of gaining so many more.

I was too shaken by my failure to carry on gambling. Instead of unloading all my money, I was now fifteen times richer than when I came in. With the money I still had in the bank, my total wealth had risen to nearly twenty million francs. One million francs a week for the rest of my life! Unless I gave up writing in order to bounce around in speedboats feeding caviar to the fish, I was never going to get rid of the wretched stuff.

I drifted into the bar, thoroughly depressed. At the same time I detected the return of that hollow acceleration, that dry-mouthed excitement, that I had noticed earlier in the evening. I wished I could just give the whole lot away, but a tramp is far harder to find in Monte Carlo than a roulette wheel. My situation was truly hopeless. Perhaps if I gambled again . . . no, that's what all the desperadoes think.

Unable to drink alcohol, which now leaves me feeling sick for days, I celebrated my defeat with Vichy water. My gloomy financial reverie was interrupted by a half-familiar voice. Turning round I saw the woman I had ravaged on the afternoon of the countess's death. The loose spirals of her golden-brown hair entangled me in nostalgia. No longer naked, we went through the introductions which our furious appetites had vaulted over. Her name, it turns out, is Angelique.

'Why don't you sit down?' she said.

'Well, it's funny you should ask,' I replied, emptying my trouser pockets, and stacking the counters up on the bar.

At least I could now move my legs freely. Only my top half felt as if I was wearing a flak jacket.

'You're having good luck tonight,' she said admiringly.

I struggled to explain how badly things were going from my point of view, but although she seemed to grasp the principle of what I was saying there was a stubborn incomprehension in her eyes each time they came to rest on the five million francs stacked up in front of us.

'I don't think you get free until you die,' she said, half-heartedly trying to participate in my preoccupations.

'If only it were that easy.' I smiled.

She had lost all her money earlier in the evening and, drawn by the inverted symmetry of our disappointments, I slid the counters along the mahogany and offered them to her.

'Lose them for me,' I said. 'I'll probably just win more.'

'You're not serious,' said Angelique.

'Absolutely serious.'

She leant over and kissed me on the mouth. 'Do you want to watch me play?' she asked, looking at me intently.

'Sure.'

Her elegant evening bag was too compact to accommodate her new fortune and, after looking around discreetly, she slipped some of the counters into her underwear, a turmoil of lace and silk, straps and buttons.

'You're *so* great,' I said, biting her earlobe. 'You drive me crazy.'

Now that I'd learned her name and was watching her play

with the desires we had merely caved into on our first meeting, I felt my passion tinged with gold, like raw liquor matured in oak. The potential for true feeling bared its teeth.

'I could fall in love with you,' I said anxiously.

'This is just the beginning,' she replied, running her nails over my unencumbered pockets.

'If I became your slave, would you set me free?' I asked.

'No,' she said, 'but you wouldn't want to be free.'

Walking back to the gambling tables, our interlocked fingers eagerly grinding each other's knuckles, I felt the charge from her warm palm throbbing through my whole body. My imagination usurped the visual field: shotguns exploding in a paint factory, wrinkled rainbows thick as cream rippling across the floor, starbursts of wet colour climbing the walls.

'Can you feel it?' she asked.

'Yes,' I said, 'yes.'

She kissed me a second time. The crowd churned around us, animated by a duller force.

And then she unlocked her fingers and turned to concentrate on the wheel. I was left transfixed by the shattering of my loneliness. I stood in a rushing stillness, which was like the smooth curve of a once turbulent soon turbulent waterfall. There could be no more violent and perfect contradiction than the agony of my relief, like the sting of blood returning to a frost-bitten limb it is already too late to save.

As I write this I am in Angelique's apartment on the Avenue Princesse Grace. She is asleep in the bedroom, while I'm sitting out on the balcony, naked under my overcoat, washed in winter sunlight. She inherited my luck last night and there are about twenty-five million francs in gambling chips scattered around the drawing room.

The fire of our love, which was like a blowtorch the first time we met, is now a burning forest, leaping rivers and consuming landscapes. She knows that I'm always thinking about death and I know that she's always longing to gamble. We reprieved each other, with every touch. With momentary impersonations, we flicked through the index cards of all our identities, and then burnt the file. There was nobody left for us to be except exactly who we are, doubly naked on an unprecedented dawn.

We didn't forget to be practical either. I am beginning a new chapter in my life. Today I am too elated to sleep, but normally we will get up in time for a late lunch at the Hôtel de Paris, and then go to the casino when it opens at four o'clock. She will take one million francs each day and gamble; I will sit in the blissfully sealed bars and restaurants of the casino, writing. Even if she loses every day, we have twenty-five delirious days together. She will make sure that I write and I will make sure that she doesn't spend more than a million francs a day. At midnight we will return and burn away our sickness in the incinerator of her bed. What more could we ask for? I feel almost religious.

12

I checked out of the Grand Large today. They told me that the hotel was dead at the moment but should revive around Easter. I'll be checking out for good by then, slipping away before *un monde fou* bears down on this strip of coast which is still beautiful enough to explain why it has been destroyed.

Even an hour's separation from Angelique dragged me into melancholy, but now that I'm back in the bar of the Salle Privée I'm in a holiday humour. I can see her through the doorway, stalking one wheel after another with a touchingly fanatical expression on her face. I am determined to continue *On the Train*, despite the fact that I feel fulfilled simply watching her move around, cocooned in the sweet oblivion of her single-mindedness, alluring in a way that only someone unconscious of being watched can be. I realize now the headlong rush into intimacy of last night's offer to let me watch her play. Gambling is what's

really private for her, and she might with comparative casualness
have offered to let me watch her masturbate.

At first I thought it was death, then consciousness; now I'm
not sure it isn't time that really fascinates me. (I read somewhere
that the deep etymology of 'fascination' is the Hittite – always
useful when there's a gap in the archaeological record – word for
vagina.) In any case they all seem tantalizingly related to one another. Identity is in there too, disappearing. There's something
that keeps changing shape but remains the same. Ways of putting it dance before me in a nervous congregation, like a cloud
of gnats at sunset, made visible by the dying light, the reddening sky.

Who wants to hear a writer complain about his impossible, his hopeless, his indissoluble, his medieval, his shotgun
marriage to words? Words distance us from the world, except of
course when they don't. Dreams are wordless, except when they
aren't. We can have a vision of the structure of the Benzene
ring, or a vision of Kubla Khan. Intuition circumvents words,
unless it lands on them. One moment we're complaining that
our very means of thought are linguistically determined, the
next that there's no language for what we've just thought.

Oh, for God's sake, let's stop being so cerebral; let's daub our
bodies in mud and stomp around on the ground, inviting Gaia
to join in our revels; let's knock back a pint of ayahuasca with
some authentic tribal persons, hurtle down the tunnel of psychedelic consciousness to the dawn of time, and drown our egos in
the white waters of the unavoidable truth. Then what? Chant?
Pray? Interpret our shamanic journeys? Write a book pissing on
Descartes? For myself, I'm grateful that thousands of years of

trouble have gone into making sense of language, especially when I'm writing.

This casino coffee certainly makes one opinionated. I'd better get on with the story.

Quite apart from an unreasonable possessiveness towards Crystal, Patrick felt some alarm at the prospect of Jean-Paul's conversation. His performance at the conference, simply entitled 'Being', took the audaciously tentative form of an 'exploration'. Jean-Paul's claim that he would 'attempt to speak *from*, and not merely *about*, the place I wish to explore' had produced long pauses in which his rapidly nodding head suggested an impressively spontaneous review of his alternatives, but also contained a hint of insanity, of the rocking chair in the back ward of the asylum. He had played with this open form by saying, after a long pause, 'So, what's next?' And then, after another pause, 'What *is* "next"?'

At this point some people had walked out, tactfully or indignantly, but others had stayed, feeling the desert plains of the future dropping away, and the bracing mental sensation of standing upright on the edge of a perpetual cliff.

Patrick realized that the latter effect could not have occurred without Jean-Paul holding himself at the point where he invited his listeners to join him. On the other hand, he sympathized with those who had come to learn something other than the impossibility of speaking accurately about what really mattered. He wondered if he could ask Crystal whether Jean-Paul was always 'like that', but she still seemed preoccupied and he hesitated for too long.

Crystal ached to be beside Peter again, or, rather, beside his body, the one place she could be sure not to find him at the moment. She couldn't have gone to Oxford if she didn't believe that her connection with him was infinitely extendable and, as the Quantum fans at the conference liked to say, 'non-local'. Two particles which had once been joined continued to influence each other after they were separated. Few people understood the physics of non-locality, but many were thrilled by its metaphoric potential.

Non-local or not, she continued to hope that consciousness would return to Peter's body, preferably while Tracy dropped a tray in the doorway, like a Victorian maid who has seen a ghost, or a bare ankle. Perhaps she could cry 'Lawksamercy' at the same time. Crystal was reluctant to deprive herself of any Pinewood effects for this moment of beneficent revenge. She quite wanted to ask Jean-Paul about non-locality, and not just for educational purposes. She didn't exactly regret going to bed with him last night – for what it was worth with her body in its current state – but she didn't want to go to bed with him tonight, and so she favoured a general conversation, possibly including this unhappy but quite intelligent man opposite.

'By the way,' she said, 'I'm Crystal.'

'Patrick.'

'Pleased to meet you,' said Crystal. 'That was Jean-Paul at the window.'

'I know,' said Patrick. 'I went to his challenging lecture. Is he always like that?'

'No. Usually he's pretentious without the long pauses,'

said Crystal. 'I'm sort of joking. He's an old boyfriend of mine.'

She knew she was being unfair to Jean-Paul. He had been so sweet to her last night, selflessly stroking her broken body, his fingertips drifting back and forth gently, like an abandoned trapeze, or tracing tortuous rivers among her cuts and bruises. He cradled the back of her head, gazing kindly into her eyes and saying, to her amazement, nothing. She hardly recognized the argumentative intellectual she had driven to psychedelic insanity in the Utah desert five years ago, the man who declared the 'scandal' of pure Being, and 'announced the death of Nature'.

'He's become much kinder,' she added, more for herself than Patrick; 'that's the main thing.'

Something horrible has just happened. I looked up from my notebook and instead of seeing Angelique in her usual rapt communion with the wheel I saw her chatting to a party of sixty-year-olds. As if this wasn't bad enough, they started to bear down in my direction.

There was an olive-brown Spaniard in an olive-green suit, who followed the inefficient policy of chuckling continuously just in case somebody made a joke. He needn't have worried. The party was led by an Italian whose rheumatic courtesies were like getting stuck behind a vintage-car rally in a narrow country lane.

A white-haired Englishwoman sighed theatrically. 'John was *so* silly not to come,' she said. 'He kept saying, "What will I do all day in La Réserve?" and I said, "What you always do: read your book and lose your cufflinks."'

'"Lose your cufflinks",' said the Spaniard. *'Maravilloso! Maravilloso!'*

'But you must remember,' said the Italian, 'for the English gentleman the cufflinks are objects of religious veneration.'

'"Religious veneration",' said the Spaniard (chuckle, chuckle).

'It is very sad that John has not been able to come on this occasion,' said the gallant Italian. 'Next time we will not let him get away so easily,' he added, duelling the air with his index finger.

A depressingly chic Frenchwoman turned to me and said, as if she were quoting Pascal, *'Je trouve qu'il fait affreusement froid ce soir.* Absolute-lay throwzen.'

'Who the fuck are these people?' I asked Angelique, dragging her aside. 'How could you let them stop you from gambling, and stop me from writing about death?'

'They're friends of mine,' she said.

'Friends?'

'Sometimes I blow all my money on the first of the month. Then I go to their dinner parties. They feed me and keep me going until the next payment arrives. Alessandro is very sweet to me.'

'Couldn't you keep some fish fingers in the deep freeze to see you through the hard times?' I sputtered.

'Fish fingers?' said Angelique, who, like so many foreigners, hadn't heard of that wonderful food. She clearly preferred Alessandro's steamed asparagus and grilled sea bass.

'Alessandro understands my little weakness. Sometimes he gives me *jetons.* I find them in my handbag after I leave. It's sweet, no?'

'It's . . .' I almost used the word prostitution, but, given that I was paying one million francs a day for her company, thought better of it. But it was not the same in my case, I was mad about her . . . maybe Alessandro was too.

Angelique said that Alessandro's party had invited us to join them in a nightclub after they had celebrated Xavier's birthday. The chuckling Spaniard is sixty today. What the hell do I care? I felt utter disgust but knew that I couldn't bear to be separated from Angelique for even a few hours.

I collapsed on a chair, knotted with jealousy.

Why is life so unsatisfactory, so disappointing? Angelique suddenly seemed ordinary and compromised, but as my general admiration for her failed, my sexual longing grew more stubborn. Jealousy was the child of this divorce: I had to possess what I was about to lose, the secret of forgetfulness, the illusion of purification.

The great thing about writing is that these troublesome emotions can just go straight onto the page. The atmosphere of imminent death is like a time-lapse movie, a slow-motion speed, pullulating with blossoms. Everything is too much. Death and writing go so well together because the unbearable everything – the chalk squealing on the blackboard, the Albinoni at full volume, the Othello-felling jealousy – can all be vaporized on the hotplate of wild indiscretion. And, at the same time, nothing changes: the chalk squeals on, the violins scrape our heartstrings, Othello dies in a pool of green blood, worrying about his reputation.

I'd better get on with the story before I'm hauled off to a nightclub.

Patrick could see Jean-Paul working his way towards them down the corridor, a wrinkled black bag on a shoulder strap, a yellow anorak with a corduroy collar, a big murky, speckled, purplish sweater, black jeans and bulbous caramel-coloured shoes. He had a hawkish face which he clearly hadn't shaved since his lecture. Just too busy having *pensées*, eh? What did Crystal want with an old boyfriend when she could have a new one? Patrick had always prided himself on not being jealous. Now he could see that he would have to throw the pride overboard and haul in the jealousy. The last thing he needed was a Lear-like eruption of self-knowledge, a busy traffic of deadly sins just as he might have expected to sink back onto the pillow in a legitimate stupor.

'Ah, just in time,' said Jean-Paul, as the train shuddered into motion. He hoisted his bag into the overhead rack and sat down next to Crystal. She introduced him to Patrick, and the two men greeted each other cautiously.

'I enjoyed your "exploration" on Saturday,' said Patrick.

Jean-Paul bowed his head. 'It was really nothing,' he said. 'At least, I hope so!'

Patrick smiled politely.

'I tried to keep it, as the English say, "short and sweet".'

'I've never understood,' Patrick drawled, 'how "short and sweet" has become a cliché when short and bitter has so much more reason to be popular.'

'But it's the shortness of the sweetness that's bitter,' said Crystal. 'So, why not stay at the source?'

'Well, thanks for clarifying that point for me, Crystal,'

said Patrick, feeling the excitement and the presumption of using her name for the first time.

'I was saving you from the in-depth perspective,' said Crystal. 'You should never begin a sentence with the words "I've never understood" when you're with Jean-Paul. He's a natural-born teacher. Which reminds me,' she said, looking at Jean-Paul teasingly, 'I've never really understood non-locality.'

'Ah, non-locality,' said Jean-Paul, as if he'd been presented with a favourite dish. 'I'm no expert, but I know a little about the territory. The traditional argument against non-locality playing any part in consciousness is that the brain is too hot and too wet for coherent quantum events to occur there. There are two ways out of this dismissal of our interesting friend. One, advanced by Penrose and Hameroff – a mathematician and an anaesthetist – is that "microtubules", the component structures of the synapses, are quantum environments sealed off from the rest of our tropical brains. These microtubules are constructed in a Fibonacci series – for a Platonist this mathematical elegance is the signature of Ideal Form. For such a temperament, it becomes irresistible to imagine a nested hierarchy linking the smallest to the greatest through the most fundamental. You can understand the temptation: the reconciliation of mysticism and science through the impersonal perfection of mathematics.

'The only other way out of the physicalist impasse is to plunge deeper into the immaterial, and lay claim to various forms of discarnate mind – the collective unconscious of Jung, or the inherent memory of Sheldrake's "morphogenetic fields". In such a model, the brain is not just the generator of consciousness but the recipient of consciousness. This lonely organ, which has appeared to be imprisoned in the skull, tormenting intellectuals throughout history,' said Jean-Paul merrily, 'may after all be a transceiver, tuning into various types of extra-physical mind, and contributing to them with its own broadcasts.'

Just as Patrick was beginning to marvel at Jean-Paul's willingness to ramble on in his survey of the field, the Frenchman fell abruptly silent.

'Well, that gets my vote,' said Crystal: 'a transceiver. It ties in with my most fundamental experiences. I don't think that ultimately we *have* consciousness, I think we just become part of it. In fact, the more we try to pretend it's ours, the less of it we have,' she went on, realizing as she voiced it that she might be overimpressed by the symmetry of this idea.

'Hang on . . .' said Patrick.

To my fury, when I finally felt that things were beginning to hot up on the train, Angelique came to tell me that it was time to go to Jimmy's nightclub with Alessandro and his party.

There I was one moment, struggling with a matter of intense personal importance, which also happens to be one of the great scientific questions of the age – the other being the origins of the universe – and the next I was in the back of Alessandro's limousine, trying not to drown in the billows of inanity which splashed over me from every direction.

'Hang on,' Patrick had said, and I could remember that he

was about to make a key point, to take us further into the laby-
rinth, but I could no longer remember what he was going to say.
I sat staring hysterically at this hiatus. 'What's next?' I might
have asked, but without Jean-Paul's playfulness. What the fuck
was next? Hang on . . . Hang on . . . Hang on for what? I had to
hang on until I was back in the casino tomorrow.

I noticed that I had, incidentally, turned into a tangential
gambling addict, unable to pursue my life's vocation except in a
casino, watching Angelique play. What had happened to Patrick's thought? Where do thoughts come from when they 'pop
up', and where do they go when they 'disappear'?

I looked at Angelique with a vehement sense of betrayal; she
looked back at me with the innocent cruelty of a baby panther.
I realized that I had attributed all kinds of passionate and
tormented reflections to her which she would never dream of
having. She really knew the trick of living in the present, from
one splash of pleasure to another. Perhaps her sexual intensity derived from her shallowness and not from the depths of tragic
knowledge I had projected on her, or perhaps this superficiality
was itself profound, born of the knowledge that everything is
surface. I no longer knew what to think, but I needed to be in
her bed, to see if I could find freedom again in her treacherous
embrace.

'After you, after you,' said Alessandro.

'I haven't been to a nightclub in yonks,' said the Englishwoman.

' "Yonks",' chuckled Xavier. *Maravilloso!*

On the dance floor, tame tax exiles tried to look wild. Big-
boned boys in blazers lassoed the air above carefully cropped

heads. Old men with tinted lenses and years of syphilis under their belts consorted with frigid models. Sharp-faced blonde girls kept their favours for the sons of Industry, and big-nosed Greek girls sat around gloomily being chaperoned by whoremongering brothers. They didn't let just anybody in.

I sat down on a velvet bench and through all the smoke and the bad music and the undesirable desire I suddenly allowed myself to become relaxed. Even here there was no need to posture. The essential question remained the same. Where could I find freedom in this situation? I looked around and felt reconciled with all the people in Alessandro's party and all the people in the room. I could spray adjectives at them for the rest of the evening, but in the end they were just people struggling to be happy with only the most unpromising material at their disposal.

'*Maravilloso*,' said Xavier.

'*Si*,' I said. '*Es maravilloso*.'

Angelique looked at me, and I could see in her eyes that she understood the breakthrough I had made. She is not only dead sexy, but probably the wisest person I've ever met.

13

'But why would a morphogenetic field have to be discarnate?' asked Patrick. 'Why couldn't it be a genetic inheritance?'

'The rapid accumulation of cultural and behavioural habits cannot be explained genetically,' said Jean-Paul, 'because the geneticists insist that behaviour does not modify the genome. Adaptation can only occur through the slow, blind process of natural selection, shaped by the accidental mutations which give a slight reproductive edge to their carriers.'

'Anyway,' said Crystal, 'the extension of the theory into "morphic resonance" completely blows the genetic connection. After the first crystallization of a solution, which may be very long and difficult, the process grows easier and easier, even in laboratories remote from each other, where no exchange of information or crystals has taken place. The solution exists in a field that is becoming increasingly grooved and tilted towards crystallization.'

'These grooves of habituation,' said Jean-Paul, 'are what Sheldrake calls "creodes".'

While Jean-Paul and Crystal tried to establish the reality of this phenomenon for Patrick, he was already preoccupied with its implications at another level. When the world was read in terms of habits, time lost its bald authority. It consisted of endlessly, organically altering textures: of crystals which formed faster and faster but, as they did so, formed more and more conservative fields, of islands of novelty erupting and then, as related habits formed around them, becoming archipelagos, stretching back towards continents of deep habit. Time itself was in an evolutionary frame. This idea pressed in on him confusedly as he tried to map it over his own subjective sense of change.

'Time looks very different,' he managed to say incoherently.

'Ah, yes,' said Jean-Paul with an appreciative smile. 'Our insistence that a second is a second is a second is a formality which may be useful for making lunch appointments, but not for understanding the true nature of reality.'

'It's not even that useful for making lunch appointments,' said Crystal.

I had to stop working to have dinner with my adorable Angelique.

The only creode I'm helping to establish is casino writing, and I hope I can make a modest contribution to literature by preparing a morphogenetic field for the next dying novelist who tries to push his plot forward in this gilded setting. Perhaps I can do more, and all over the world, to the despair of their managers, casinos will start to fill with coughing authors, stooped over their notebooks or holding X-rays up to the chandeliers and neon flamingos to remind themselves why they can't afford to stop working.

Before we had dinner, Angelique lost another half million. Ten of our twenty-five million is gone, and if her luck doesn't change we only have another fifteen days together. Some people might think it pedantic not to carry on after the money has run out, and for a while I found myself wavering on this point, but Angelique is right to be adamant. There might seem to be something touchingly human about spending the last four months of my life with the woman I love, being reassured, being nursed (when she's not at the casino), introducing her to fish fingers; but imagine the mediocrity of such a resignation after we have strapped ourselves to the wheel, after we have distilled time in the retort of our unbreakable contract, so that each moment we spend together falls, drop by drop, like liquid fire on to our outstretched and writhing tongues.

Yes, Angelique is definitely right. Besides, she might win, and then our extraordinary happiness will hold.

I try to challenge that happiness to see if it is false. Am I wedding myself to Fortune because it is the unreliable sidekick of a reliably nasty Fate? Parting from Angelique is almost as terrifying as death, and yet I expect to survive it. Am I using her as a training ground for extinction, manfully putting the pistol to my temple and firing a blank?

No, on the contrary, the two endings enhance each other: leaving her body and leaving my own body have become as beautifully entwined as entering her body with my body.

Walking here from her apartment, I saw aqueducts of rainbows arching down the polluted avenues. I was ready to die because I was entirely fulfilled, and I was ready to live because I was entirely ready to die. I had never felt less indifferent to life or more indifferent to death. This moment could not have occurred at any other moment, nor could it occur again at any other moment. We walked in silence until we had almost arrived, and then Angelique turned to me and said, 'What a feeling,' and we kissed on the steps of the casino.

Time may pass quickly when you're having fun, but when you're happy it almost stops. Heavily freighted as Cleopatra's barge, it can't be expected to flit along. All ideas and all impressions are accepted by a mind with no motive to shut down. The more conscious I am, the slower time moves. The toll is that I have to stay conscious of death, but if I insisted on 'having fun' instead, I would hurtle down a wall of ice towards the very thing I was trying to forget. Standing on the steps of the casino, I thought of saying to Angelique that if we want to slow down the approach of death we must entertain it ceaselessly, but she knows that already; it's only thanks to her that I'm realizing it at all.

As I begin to experience more freedom, the definition of what it is changes. Freedom is always what I don't have, because it refuses to be possessed. It may have a 'field', though, in which I can learn to spend more time, and for that I can never thank Angelique enough.

I suppose I'll have to burden my characters with more ru-

minations on this subject. I need to place my own feverishly tex-
tured sense of time in some scientific framework other than
hallucination. Fiction, of course, textures time in its own way
and superimposes further layers of elasticity and roughness. One
character can assess the meaning of her entire life, while another,
apparently caught in a world of molasses, just manages to light
a cigarette during the same period. Dialogue gives us a bracing
sense of honesty because it appears to take place over the same
duration as the rest of life. The characters would take as long to
speak what they say outside a book as they do within it. On the
other hand, we are reading and not listening and, with any luck,
what they have to say is less diffuse than most conversation, and
therefore artificially compressed.

So, what am I going to do with these characters of mine? It
might not be implausible for their train to break down at Didcot. If it speeds its way to London uninterrupted, they only have
fifty-five minutes to solve the riddle of consciousness, an unfair
pressure to put on any conversation.

I've just seen my darling Angelique collect a stack of
100,000-franc counters. That means that I have a while before
we go back to her apartment. It's tempting to eliminate dialogue
from the next section of *On the Train*, to ruffle the smooth surface of equal duration, to plunge into a speculating or remembering mind while the rest of the world achieves almost nothing.

'We can't already be in Didcot,' said Patrick.

'We may not have time to crack the code before we arrive
at Paddington,' said Crystal.

'We could be going to Vladivostok and still get nowhere

if we refuse to look into the heart of the matter,' said Jean-Paul.

'And what's that, *monsieur le professeur*?' said Crystal.

'Dualism!' said Jean-Paul.

'That old chestnut.'

'Two old chestnuts,' Jean-Paul corrected her.

'If we're going to have two, we might as well have three – a soul as well as a mind and body.'

'No, no,' said Jean-Paul, 'two chestnuts is more than enough, I assure you. My terrible confession is that I am convinced by certain philosophical arguments which dissolve in the light of my own experience, but which I would nevertheless like to resolve in their own terms.'

'But if the terminology of the arguments is inadequate for your experience, why not chuck it out?' said Patrick impatiently.

'Ultimately I do,' said Jean-Paul, 'but penultimately I would like to convince some of those who occupy my abandoned positions that they should abandon them as well.'

'You're a missionary,' said Crystal.

'Yes, I'm afraid so,' said Jean-Paul, opening his hands in a plea for clemency.

'I knew a philosopher called Victor Eisen,' said Patrick, 'who worked on the problem of identity. Nobody knew better who he could properly be said to be if half his body happened to be replaced by Greta Garbo's, which it wasn't, by the way; or his partially damaged brain was transplanted into a robot's body after three hundred years in a cryogenic vat. His autobiography, on the other hand, is dry and shallow, because he forgot to pay attention to the experience of being alive.'

'That is not a problem confined to philosophers,' said Jean-Paul. 'The question is *what* attention do we pay to the experience of being alive. Is it necessarily dualistic?'

'Or troilistic.' Crystal smiled. 'You know my woefully simple position on this question, namely, that our perceptions and sensations are indeed dualistic, but that they needn't be. We can experience non-duality.'

'Yes, I do know your position,' said Jean-Paul, bowing to her in the Indian style.

'I would go further,' she went on, 'and say that we should make those peaks of non-dual experience into the ground of our being.'

'You call that a simple position!' said Jean-Paul, looking genuinely shocked.

'And my simple position,' said Patrick, 'is that we can make our experience as fragmented as we like, but that it isn't a flaw in reality, just a fault in the transceiver.'

'And yet that advances nothing, because we then have to know whether the fault is inherent to the transceiver,' said Jean-Paul. 'Is it a dualistic transceiver?'

'Ladies and gentlemen,' an announcement came over the system. 'Due to circumstances beyond our control . . .'

'Fucking Didcot,' muttered Patrick. 'Why does one always get stuck in Didcot? And in the fog.'

14

I haven't been able to write for several days. Not only did Angelique continue to lose money, but she managed to get rid of several million in one evening. She found the place where I used to hide the gambling counters and took a few more million after I had given her the evening's supply. She was very brazen about it the next day. I almost felt that she wanted to get rid of me, the way one sometimes tries to hasten the unbearable. I argued that I was owed the days that she overspent, and she counter-argued that my job was to stop her gambling all the money at once and that the terms of our contract couldn't be altered just because I had failed. We started bickering. She became imperious and remote, while I dropped defencelessly into depression.

Although the liver is nerveless, I had been warned to expect some 'discomfort' from pressure on the intestines as well as 'referred liver pain' under the right shoulder blade. Among the endless medical complications I might expect, the most exotic was the cirrhotic liver's failure to eliminate the small amount of oestrogen naturally produced by a man, causing my breasts to swell painfully. The prospect of drifting towards a biochemical womanhood was not altogether displeasing, but I couldn't adjust to the fact that I would only be able to sleep on my back. There would also be 'magnified mood swings', 'blackness', and 'impaired memory' to contend with.

And yet, over the last two months I'd been miraculously, almost disturbingly, free of symptoms. In fact I was growing more vital every day. Until we started arguing, love and work seemed to enable me to transcend my physical limitations, but then all the symptoms pounced at once, like wild animals when the camp fires die out in the middle of the night.

I had to retire to bed. I had a spear in my side and a trowel digging under my shoulder blade; hatpins of brief agony shot through my body unpredictably. My vision blurred and my jaundiced eyeballs and coated tongue spoke of imminent catastrophe. I started to forget the names of my characters and lost any sense of their respective personalities. Angelique, moving around in the neighbouring rooms, trampled on my aching body. Breathing in, reputedly an instinct, became a negotiated settlement.

And still I handed the haughty and faintly disgusted Angelique her daily gambling money, the high price of my suicide-inducing bed and breakfast. Each time she came in and held out her impatient hand, close enough to reach the counters but too far for me to catch her wrist and pull her over to my side, I thought of *le père* Goriot, bedridden in his filthy garret but only wishing he could be further exploited by his marble-hearted daughters.

Yesterday Angelique came into the bedroom holding my thin manuscript. She moved towards the open window and I surged up from the pillows shouting, 'Don't!'

'Oh, don't worry,' she said, 'I'm not going to throw it out of the window – that would be doing you a favour.'

'You don't like it?'

'It's wooden and dry and boring. I can't believe this is what you want to do with your last days. Why don't you write about how wonderful the figs taste when you know you may never taste one again?'

'Because they don't,' I said, 'they taste like ash.'

'Why don't you tell us how we must live every moment to the full because life is so precious?'

'Because if it's dying that makes you realize that, you're already too anxious to do anything about it. I wanted to do something serious . . .'

'You are doing something serious: you're dying,' she said, laughing.

'Something impersonal.'

'But that's exactly the problem: you must make it more personal, more human, more dramatic. You should write from your own experience, write about *us*.' She put the manuscript on the table by the window. 'I'm only trying to help,' she said. 'I think the real problem is that you don't know how to make abstract ideas exciting. You should read Alain. We used to read him in the Lycée. He's wonderful. After a page of Alain, you see Spinoza everywhere.'

'I'll check him out,' I said feebly.

She left the room and, paralysed by failure and confusion, I watched the breeze scatter the pages across the floor.

On my third day in bed Angelique let me know, with some reluctance, that we'd been invited to lunch by a friend of Alessandro's who had a fabulous house in the hills above Cap d'Ail. Where was that largesse I'd felt at Jimmy's? Gone. I loathed the idea of the lunch party, but I couldn't bear Angelique to drift further from me, to make the reanimation of our perfect love yet more impossible, and so I excavated myself from the bed and, assembling the fragments of a social identity, set off with her in the back of one of Alessandro's cars, obsessively fingering my aching new breasts, like a thirteen-year-old girl.

Our convoy of limousines glided down the long drive, past deeply shaded lawns, and arrived at a seventeenth-century chateau the colour of lavender honey, with pale-grey shutters. We parked beside a gurgling trout pond, its reflected light trembling steadily on the jasmine-crowded walls of an old tower. Angelique, for whom the house represented rather less than a month's gambling in an inconveniently solid form, was less impressed than I was. I found it the perfect setting for the war between dignity and self-pity which was raging inside me. Heaving myself out of the car, I imagined the soundtrack that might accompany the long shots of a dying man walking along those gravel paths. A close-up of an intelligent and passionate face. The scream of a peacock counterpointing its own visual charm and piercing through the aesthetic consolations of the place. Yes, a peacock, the symbol of immortality, turned into the messenger of death. I thought of the Maestro and the balance he would have kept between the wit of the treatment and the savagery of the subject.

And then one of those extraordinary things happened. Our host came out of the house and before he even greeted us he cried out, 'The Maestro is dead. It's a tragedy for the cinema.'

'But I was just thinking about him,' I stammered stupidly.

Pamela, the white-haired Englishwoman, leant over to me confidentially and said, 'John can't stand his films; says they're "pretentious twaddle".'

I looked at her with hatred, but she was too pleased with her quotation to notice.

'He died behind the camera,' said Jean-Marc, pausing on the steps of his house.

'Ah, *bravissimo!*' said Alessandro.

'I'm sure it's how he would have wanted to go,' said Pamela. 'Captain going down with his ship and all that.'

'He was working on a film called *Flat*,' said Jean-Marc.

'Only the Maestro . . .' murmured Alessandro admiringly.

'Alas, it was incomplete when he died, but there will be a screening in Cannes this May. I happen to be on the festival committee,' Jean-Marc hurried past the glamour of his connections, 'and I thought we should form a party.'

There was a babble of approval.

'I'll be dead by May,' I said quietly.

'Oh, no, not you as well,' said Pamela. 'What a morbid lunch.'

'But surely you wouldn't want to miss it,' said Jean-Marc, placing his hand lightly on my back as he guided me into the hall. 'Alessandro tells me you're in the cinema yourself.'

'We're all in the cinema,' I said, influenced, perhaps, by Pamela's mention of 'pretentious twaddle'.

'Ah, yes,' said Jean-Marc.

'What does it mean, "we're all in the cinema"?' said the chic Frenchwoman indignantly. 'I never go to the cinema. For me it is absolute-lay a nightmare to be locked in the dark with all the ordinary people.'

'Of course I don't want to miss it . . .' I went on.

'Well, then, it's decided,' said Jean-Marc, resuming control after a crisis of defection: 'we can count on you to come.'

Two greyhounds with red leather collars sat beneath their own portrait in a hall that smelt of wood smoke and lilies.

'My cook is furious with me,' Jean-Marc confessed, 'because, as a homage to the Maestro, I asked her to prepare a lunch based on the famous scene in *Pompeii* where they feast on oysters and suckling pig. The shellfish were not a problem, but she had to hunt high and low to find the suckling pig.'

Everyone agreed that only Jean-Marc would have gone to such trouble.

In the drawing room Jean-Marc's wife, dressed in cream linen edged with black velvet, stood beside the fireplace like a funeral invitation. Her eyelids drooped almost to closure and her long pale body did its best to resemble the lilies which overflowed from every vase. She greeted us with unaffected indifference. The house had belonged to Marie-Louise's father, Jean-François de Hauteville, as she was inclined to remind her husband and other visitors. Everything that Marie-Louise touched or refused to touch was in the very best taste. She looked over my shoulder as if admiring a landscape which had just been painted for her by

Poussin and in which I was not included. Even the burglars who had robbed the chateau earlier that year had been 'real professionals' with 'very good taste'. Had they been ordinary thugs, without degrees in art history, they could never have been admitted to Marie-Louise's circle.

The Maestro's death was not likely to impress her when a member of her own family had died only last week. It had been her 'disagreeable duty' to go to the family vaults in Cannes and remove the remains of the old Admiral de Hauteville in order to make room for the new arrival. When the Admiral's tomb was opened, there was nothing inside. The remains had not remained. *Vanité des vanités, tout est vanité.* Only Bossuet could have done justice to the depths of the loss, but Bossuet, it went without saying, was dead. Saying that things went without saying and saying them anyway was, in Marie-Louise's opinion, sophisticated. When she strayed from this policy it was in order to say things which were plainly absurd.

'I don't know a painter or a writer who hasn't known what they want to do by the age of two,' she explained, when we were discussing the Maestro's mythologizing of his cinematic destiny.

'The world will never be the same again without the Maestro,' Alessandro concluded.

'My dear Alessandro, the world never is the same again,' said Marie-Louise, 'with or without the Maestro.'

While we chomped our oysters and suckling pig, I noticed that a strange mood had overtaken Angelique, a mood of such vehement boredom that, had we been in a Buñuel movie, she would have turned out to be a terrorist and the lunch party would have ended explosively. I asked her as soon as possible if everything was all right.

'I can't stand that stuck-up bitch,' she said. 'Let's go for a walk in the garden.'

We went outside while the others drank coffee, and plunged deep into the grounds. When we were well hidden from the house, Angelique leant against the rough bark of an old umbrella pine and let out a growl of fury and contempt.

'Fuck me,' she said angrily.

My symptoms melted away as I unzipped my trousers. Clasping her buttocks, I hoisted her off the ground and entered her standing up. She groaned as her back grated against the trunk; I wept with gratitude to be back inside her.

Soon my arms felt as if they were being torn from their sockets.

'My arms,' I moaned.

'My back, you're tearing the skin off my back,' she replied.

We fell over slowly, trying not to disconnect. I lay on my back in a bed of pine needles and Angelique, her skirt hoisted up and pinned back by her elbows, and her fingers pushing aside the complications of her underwear, looked down at me with that febrile pensiveness which absorbs every inflection of physical pleasure. She drew the heat up through the centre of her body, like hot mercury in a thermometer, bursting the glass, streams of quicksilver running down her sides and bathing us in brilliant danger. It felt like the first time and the last time, the double ecstasy of a fatal renewal.

'Oh, no, that bitch has followed us,' said Angelique, looking through the trees at the lawn.

'We'd better stop,' I said with a sigh.

'No, I refuse to let her stop us. You're my prisoner,' she said, pinning my arms down and making small but telling movements with her hips, rolling them one way and then another, clenching and unclenching her muscles.

'Don't be absurd,' I gasped. 'We can't be caught like this.'

I could hear their voices now, without being able to make out what they were saying. How could I explain our predicament? To which scene in the Maestro's repertoire were we alluding?

Angelique leant forward slowly, arching her spine inwards as she pushed back, our foreheads touching and our eyes intercrossed. Our bellies and our chests joined, our noses brushed, our lips met and our tongues slithered confidently over each other. She sprang back and fixed me in the eye. It was almost too strong. My mind floated like the Bullet Train above its tracks, meeting no obstruction; everything clear.

'Ah, there you are,' said Marie-Louise, without any particular emphasis. 'My father used to call this the "Lovers' Grove". I'm happy to see that the tradition is being kept alive.'

I strained back and managed to say, 'It's the garden scene from *The Roads of Venice*.'

'Ah, *bravissimo*,' said Alessandro.

'*Je trouve que c'est très réussi*,' said Jean-Marc. 'A great suquecess.'

'Now I can see why they didn't want any coffee,' said Pamela, in the tone of someone who knows she is being witty.

'We all pay homage to the Maestro in our own way,' I said, hoping to bring the interview to an end.

Angelique let out a cry of joy. 'I'M COME-ING!' she shouted. 'OH, GOD, IT'S SO GOOD, IT'S SO GOOD!'

'Shall we go and see the pagoda?' said Marie-Louise, leaving us in no doubt that orgasms, properly speaking, should be silent.

We didn't bother to go back to the house, but walked down to the main road, kissing and laughing and brushing debris from each other's clothes and hair. We hitched our way back to Monte Carlo and were in the casino by half-past four.

The fever is back. Our love is stronger than ever. We have only five days of gambling money left. Time is running out, screaming. I can see Angelique drifting among the tables, scattering treasure as she goes. Her glances light gunpowder trails between us, and as she turns back to the wheel the feel of her erupts inside me.

At last I can get back to writing.

'Sometimes,' drawled Patrick, as he marvelled at the pearly bruise of fog splintering the station lights, 'I suffer from a fit of misguided simplicity. I think that the brain and the mind are aspects of the same thing, that there is no mind–body problem, any more than there's a car wheel problem. The problem is our passion for making convenient distinctions which we then treat as if they had an independent reality.

'What if everything is as it appears to be? What if consciousness is an aspect of the mind, the mind a redescription of the brain and the brain a part of the body, and they are all interdependent, with no epiphenomenon, no duality, no discarnate minds?

'Anyhow, I have these fits,' Patrick concluded, drawing a spiral in the condensation of the window, 'but I soon recover, and if I don't I cancel everything and get myself to the nearest consciousness conference. After that, it's only a matter of minutes before this pathetic vision of integrity shatters into a thousand "problems".'

'You had me convinced there for a moment,' said Crystal. 'I'm a sucker for that down-home, plain man's wisdom.'

They smiled at each other and Patrick felt a wave of happiness. He wanted to play with Crystal, to talk with her about the most abstract and the most intimate things, to visit places with her, to make love to her, to make love to her right now. He could kneel on the floor and bury his head in her lap, and forget that he was dying. He could kiss her bruised body with unspeakable tenderness, concentrating all the love which he had somehow never found it convenient to donate to a starving world. He was ready to give it now. He radiated this feeling in Crystal's direction while continuing to admire the damp iridescence of the station lamps.

Crystal felt the warm blast of his attention, which was like stepping out of a plane into a tropical country. After all the Tantric sex courses she had attended with Peter she was nothing if not open-minded, but, caught between an unconscious husband and a revived ex-boyfriend, she felt unable to take on this newcomer with his heavy charge of troubled desire. And yet there was something touching about him – that combination of defiance and vulnerability, not trapped in the restless shuffle of adolescence, but held in a kind of oppressed balance, like two caryatids shouldering a slab of stone. And beneath that – the ground they stood on – she could feel an inconsolable sadness.

'Do you think anybody lives in Didcot,' said Patrick, 'or is it just for getting stuck in?'

'If you get stuck long enough, the distinction wears thin,' said Crystal.

'Exactly,' said Patrick. 'There are probably thousands of residents who just happen to live on trains.'

Jean-Paul had dropped out of the conversation, like a swimmer who breathes out and allows himself to sink to the bottom of a pool, resting a while in the peaceful interval between landing and needing to breathe again. Patrick's muddled physicalist apology and his banter with Crystal reached him like the muffled sounds and distorted shapes of poolside action. And yet he knew exactly what was going on above the surface. He was not engaging with what was being said, but he was not ignoring it either. He was just resting. Not all the theories in the world could stop him from resting.

The slow metallic drumbeat of the tracks and the screech of braking wheels announced the arrival of another train. The fog swirled and scattered, and reassembled as the dark-blue carriages drew to a halt at the neighbouring platform.

'Ah,' said Patrick, 'so that's why we've been made to wait. It's the royal train. Who knows which member of that legendary family is jumping the queue?'

'But if we've stopped for them,' said Crystal, 'why have they stopped as well?'

'This is a parliamentary democracy,' said Patrick. 'Even the royal family have to acknowledge the paralysing influence of Didcot Junction.' And then, feeling the encroachment of another fit of simplicity, he started to argue again.

'Why are we so astonished by consciousness? When my hand feels my leg, I'm not amazed that it feels itself at the same time. Why be amazed that the mind, while receiving sense data, also receives data about itself?'

'The Buddhists treat the heart–mind as a sixth sense,' said Crystal, 'abolishing that little problem as well as a number of others.'

'How sensible,' said Patrick.

'Exactly. Consciousness is in the senses – all six of them. Awareness is just the measure of how unobstructed a relationship we have with making sense.'

'That is not the problem,' Jean-Paul sighed, unable to go on enjoying his rest.

'Oh, my God,' said Crystal, 'the professor has woken. Being aware is not the problem?'

'Of course, of course, you know you have made me into a Being freak. But in order to define consciousness, we need to pause before we arrive at the enticing word "awareness", this mermaid who appears to have human form until we embrace her and she takes us down into the luminous depths in which you are so beautifully at home.'

'Well, gee,' said Crystal.

'For you the problem is how to keep your consciousness expanded – what facilitates and frustrates that task. What we must do, however much we sympathize with your mermaid's progress towards awareness of awareness or the presence of absence, is to look at a very banal act of consciousness, the apprehension of sense data.'

'Oh, let's not look at a banal act,' said Crystal.

'Anyway, how banal is it?' said Patrick. 'We bring the whole history of our formation to what we see. If we're lucky, after years of meticulous analysis we may be able to prise open a little gap and interrupt the glibness of the projection, but we'll still be struggling with the fact that what we see is a selection made by how we feel.'

'Stop!' said Jean-Paul. 'Let's not stray down that route either. Let us leave aside the psychoanalytic, the Buddhistic, the question of scientific method, the paranormal, the linguistic . . .' Jean-Paul started to smile at Crystal's indignant face.

'So what aren't we setting aside?'

'The fact that we have no idea how a single event could have physiological and phenomenal properties at the same time, no idea how consciousness results from irritated tissue or firing neurons. This mind–body problem is not trivial. A correlation is not a cause. Cerebral activity and consciousness may occur at the same time, but until we know how they interact they will lead parallel lives. I just ask you to appreciate their philosophical isolation.'

'Of course we appreciate it,' said Crystal sympathetically, as if she was talking to a child who had cut his finger.

Jean-Paul noticed the 'we' more keenly than he would have liked.

'Oh, look, they're off,' said Patrick.

The dark-blue carriages of the royal train slipped into the fog, but still their own train remained immobile in the empty station.

15

I managed to write those last few pages since our lunch at Jean-Marc's, but now I've been taken over by my circumstances and can't carry on.

Yesterday was my last day with Angelique. I suggested we go to the Grand Large, where we first met, and although she agreed she could barely disguise her impatience with my sentimentality. The casino is only ten yards east of the Hôtel de Paris, where we usually have lunch, and it clearly irked her to be driven dozens of miles in the wrong direction by someone whose credit was about to run out. I was mortified that we were reduced to commenting listlessly on our food, like a couple of alienated pensioners in whom enthusiasm, even for mutual torment, has been entirely replaced by the congealing powers of resignation and habit. In other words, like the rest of the clientele. By the time my *myrtilles Metternich* arrived I was furious.

'What makes you think that I'm going to give you my last million francs when all you can do is sit there sulking?'

'We have a contract,' she said.

'Yes, but it's based on passion. Without passion it's shit.'

'I know you're under pressure with your health and everything,' she said politely, 'and it's difficult for both of us that we're separating tomorrow morning,' she soldiered on, 'but I think it's unfair of you to start threatening me just because you feel bad. You know I have to gamble, so if you're not going to give me the money I'm going to go to the bank right now before it closes. I'll leave your bags with the hall porter.'

'You "have to gamble". You think you're so wild and haunted, don't you? But your life is as routine as a bank clerk's, except that your mission is to throw away as much money as you can, which isn't, in some cases, the aim of bank employees.'

'Fuck you,' she growled. 'You have no idea what it means to take risks.'

'Bullshit! You're the one who's playing safe. For you, danger is removed to a world of tokens and substitutes. Why gamble with chips and cards when you can play with your life and sanity? The answer is that you don't dare.'

'I know you're unhappy because you're going to die soon, but you don't have to take it out on me,' said Angelique. She picked her bag off the floor and slid her chair back from the table.

I suddenly felt the chasm of her departure. 'Don't go,' I said, clasping her forearm. I took out my last two 500,000-franc tokens and put them on the table. 'I'm upset, that's all. I can't bear the idea of our parting. It's . . .' I stopped, knowing that we couldn't have that conversation again. 'Listen, I'm going to go for a walk now. I'll see you back home or in the Salle Privée.'

'OK, darling,' she said, kissing my hand, and struggling to load her handbag with the huge rectangles of shining plastic. 'It's so silly to argue on our last precious day together.'

I left the hotel and set off round the coastal path of St Jean-Cap-Ferrat, feeling overwhelming anguish at the prospect of being separated from Angelique. I had to keep up a hot pace so as to turn the feeling of being overwhelmed into one of being pursued; if I was pursued perhaps I could escape. But I couldn't escape. The fear was in my marrow.

What was the fear in the marrow? The loss of Angelique and, behind that, the loss of the illusion that she cared for me.

And behind the illusion that she cared for me, the knowledge that my mother had not cared for me, that she had never overcome the feeling that a baby was in bad taste. She spent the first years of my life at a careful distance, her eyes closed and a scented handkerchief pressed to her nostrils. Later on she tried to instruct me in the good taste which enabled her to find me repulsive in the first place. No wonder I had noticed Marie-Louise. Everything was falling into place.

I cursed the compulsion which had driven me to spend my time soliciting the love of a woman who has no love to give. The reason Angelique had fooled me was that she never attempted to: she had left the deception to me. Had she pretended, I would have seen through her, but what I could not see through was my own deepest longings. How does that happen? How can we choose not to know what we cannot help knowing? How could

I write about consciousness without writing about the fear in the marrow, the fear of loveless desolation which was laying waste the last months of my life?

I couldn't walk fast enough to keep ahead of the vicious panic which filled every cell in my body, and every possible world I could imagine, chasing me round the Cap like one of the *chiens méchants* advertised on every gatepost. I was on the edge, no longer playing with metaphors or describing states of mind, but stumbling along a twisting coastal path, the sea sirening me to slip, or more candidly, to dive, on to the rocks. I imagined my blood mingling with the sea; wondered how little time it would take for the salt and the sun to bleach my corpse. Would the crabs feasting on my brain find themselves, as they sucked the morsels of Broca's area or Wernicke's area from their busy claws, troubled by the problem of consciousness, or burdened by the need to finish *On the Train*? It seemed no more likely than my wanting to fulfil the aspirations of the langoustines I had for lunch. But perhaps I was fulfilling their aspirations. Perhaps that's what made me want to dive off the cliff back into the sea. Mad thoughts. Sparks from the wheel.

I slowed down and tried to return to the thing which these thoughts were scattering from: the fear in the marrow. Is there any negotiation with the feelings stitched into our growing bones, the things we knew before our first set of teeth?

I suddenly saw with a strange clarity, a clarity which took me deeper into confusion, a glass knot, saw that I could only make any difference to the terror of loveless desolation by penetrating its chaotic heart. If I could consciously live what I could not bear I might be able to reshape it. I glimpsed a molten core

to consciousness, a protean heat where everything could be re-
shaped. Yes, a molten core, like the core of the earth, deeper than
the deposits of civilization, beyond the complacencies of archae-
ology. I grabbed the air, closing my fist on this elusive vision.

I remembered that at the beginning of my gambling phase
I had only wanted to throw away half my capital. I still had 1.2
million francs in the bank. If I gave another million to Angelique I could buy one more day in her fantastic company. I could
annihilate the simulacrum of our intimacy, and return to the
truly harrowing intimacy of solitude. First it was Prozac I had
to give up; now it was Angelique. I might appear to be acting
from panic, like a rabbit dashing under the wheels of the car it
dreads, or merely expressing my fear of separation by buying another day, but I would in fact be purifying myself of a fear which
distorted everything. I would give away my last million in order to
savour the pathology of my motives, second by second; volunteer-
ing for the Chinese water torture of an unbearable knowledge.

Indifferent to the jogger who panted his way towards me on
the coastal path, I let out a scream of fury. I was swaying with
vertigo and blazing with conviction at the same time, knowing
that I was taking a mad gamble, but knowing that if I didn't I
would lose everything.

16

Things haven't worked out quite as I envisaged on Cap Ferrat. What on earth did I think I was doing? Not content with a month of sick love, I have pushed myself to the brink of destitution by insisting on another day. Not only did I give away my last whole million, but instead of the two hundred thousand francs I expected to have left, I found one hundred and eight. I forgot to cancel the direct debits on my household expenses and that scumbag Dai Varey has been on the phone to Australia ever since, with all the lights on and the hot water running. If my doctor turns out to be wrong, things could get very nasty. As it is, I only have just enough for four months. I must stop asking for a quarter bottle of Evian with my coffee. That'll be a saving. I can't help being scandalized by an indiscriminate tax like VAT which hits rich and poor alike.

Mind you, inspiration can't fail to strike under these

miserable conditions. I've achieved poverty and isolation, the world-famous formula for artistic success, among other things.

I'm in a *pension* in the red-light district of Toulon. The wallpaper must have been brought here from Oscar Wilde's death chamber. In this case, however, it's not clear which one of us will go first. The building next door is being demolished and a ball and chain could easily slip through the emaciated walls at any moment. In the meantime, and what a mean time it is, brown and purple flowers with the texture of warts press in from every side of my tiny room. At the slightest movement my bed twangs like an unstrung guitar.

Outside, the French genius for covering pavements in dog shit achieves its most perfect expression, leaving almost no room for the beggars to display their cardboard autobiographies. As darkness rushes tactfully onto the streets, hideous women, sometimes overweight, sometimes dangerously thin, offer parts of their bodies for rent at understandably modest prices.

I wish I could stay but I've heard of a beautiful island nearby where the off-season rates are even more reasonable than they are here. I've found a room through an advertisement in the *Var Matin*, looking after the summer house of a Toulon family. I went for an interview and they seemed to think that it was pleasingly romantic to have an *écrivain anglais* caretaking for them. I'll be living on the wild side of Porquerolles, a carless, unbuilt miracle of preservation, so they tell me. I can walk to the village to buy my supplies and then go home to write *On the Train*. I am hoping my life will be perfectly uneventful, so that I can concentrate exclusively on my novel. My last day in Monte Carlo, by contrast, was far from uneventful and I'll have to describe it as briefly as possible so my mind is clear enough to carry on with the work.

I returned from my cliffside vision convinced that I had glimpsed a state in which I could become free through the intensity of my self-consciousness, and through being the neutral witness of my pathology. It turned out not to be so easy to pack decades of psychotherapy into one day of deliberate unhappiness. I did my best.

The first thing that threw me when I went back to Angelique's apartment was the letter waiting for me in the hall from my implacably literary friend Lola.

My dear Charles,

Imagine how delighted I was to hear that you've been *spotted*, pen in hand, in the Monte Carlo casino. They'll have to put up a plaque! I happen to be on Jean-Marc Olivier's committee for the screening of *Flat*, the Maestro's unfinished masterpiece (which, by the way, is absolutely marvellous and in some mysterious way better, and truer to itself, for being *unfinished*. One could almost think he died for aesthetic reasons, Maestro to the last). Anyhow, our mutual friend says that you've been creating quite a stir by beavering away in the Salle Privée while your engaging-sounding Muse loses huge sums of money at the tables. Please reassure me that you're not just adding up her losses!

Oh, Charles, how wonderful if you're finally getting down to the serious work I know you have inside you. One can't help thinking of Dr Johnson's famous remark!

If there's anything I can do to help, you know I'm only too willing. I'll be staying at Jean-Marc's all week. Do ring me if you have a moment when you're quite certain you can't write another word.

Lots of love and tons of admiration for your courage,

Lola

I was writhing with irritation. How could I be expected to concentrate on the root fear under these circumstances? I wrote a short sarcastic note inviting Lola to be my literary executor and assuring her that if I died before my novel was finished it would not be for aesthetic reasons.

I had scarcely finished when the phone rang. I answered it, in case it was Angelique.

'Hello.'

'Hi, baby, it's Heidi!'

'Heidi, how did you find me?'

'Lola told me your number.'

'What would I do without that woman?' I muttered.

'Don't be grumpy, you silly billy,' said Heidi. 'I'm ringing with good news.'

'Oh, yeah?'

'I want you to see Ton Len.'

'You do?'

'I didn't realize you were really ill,' she said.

'Did you think I was lying?'

'I thought it was some kind of English joke,' she said, laughing as merrily as one of the mountain streams that crowd her native land. 'You know the way I never got your sense of humour.'

'How could I forget?'

'I think it's important for Ton Len to have some photos of herself with her daddy, and when she's older we can look at them together and I'll tell her what a wonderful man you were.'

'That'll be nice,' I said, wondering if things could get any worse.

We made some practical arrangements, and Heidi drew the conversation gracefully to a close. 'I've got a Tibetan monk doing a ritual for you, so you can die more consciously.'

'Don't use that word. I never want to hear it again.'

'You can go into the Bardo state fully aware of what's happening,' chirped Heidi, like a mystic wind-up doll. 'It's incredible. You can have a proactive relationship with your next birth.'

'You really shouldn't have gone to all that trouble.'

'It's nothing,' she said. 'I also want you to know that I've worked through my issues around us and I totally forgive you.'

'For what?'

'Everything,' she said, blowing me a kiss down the line.

I could hardly find room to accommodate what was going on. See my daughter? See her now? Was it too late? Never too late for a photo shoot.

In the bedroom there was a letter for me on the pillow, this time from Angelique.

My darling,

I'm sorry we had such a horrible lunch. It's all my fault. I find myself faltering as we approach the moment when we must separate. I cannot bear to lose you. I have never known a passion like ours. I have never given myself so completely. It's very hard for me, I've always been so frightened of getting close to anyone. I've never told you this before, but both my parents were killed in a car accident when I was three. I was always told what a 'terrible misfortune' it was, and ever since I have been fascinated by bad luck. I gamble in order to get close to Maman and Papa. Only by losing can I enter the mysterious absence which constitutes their love.

Don't you see that I cannot let you stay, I cannot fall more in love with you when you will soon be dead. It's not the money, my darling, it's just that I've found a system for coping with my unhealable wound and I cannot allow you to destroy that system when you will not be here to hold me among the ruins.

Let's come back early tonight and make love as never before. Now you know my terrible secret, make love to it, go to the heart of it, make love to my wound with your own desperate desire to live and then let's part before the dawn, like the two vampires we really are, belonging more to death than life; let's not wait for the beams of the reproachful sun to discover us together, staining our love-soaked sheets with tears.

Come to me soon, my darling. I long to be with you.

Angelique

Of course I didn't believe a word of it. Still, I felt an involuntary stiffening in my trousers. I was sure that if I hunted around the flat I would find the prototype of this letter, customized for each bankrupt lover. It was too smoothly written not to be rehearsed. I couldn't help admiring the way she proposed to get rid of me before breakfast.

I paced around the room indignantly rereading the letter. Then the terrifying possibility that she was telling the truth stabbed through my contempt, like a dagger through an arras. Even if the letter was carefully written, that didn't mean it wasn't true. Authenticity doesn't have to be inarticulate. What if my own root fear (which I was now over-fearlessly confronting) made me want to believe she was a cold, selfish bitch, when in fact she was someone who couldn't afford to love me any more than she did? I started to spiral as I attempted to catch sight of the distorting effect of my proudly unveiled terror. How could I see through my fear without looking through it at the same time? I was already lost and I hadn't even proposed an extra day to Angelique.

Needless to say, as Marie-Louise would say, things didn't improve when I arrived at the casino. Angelique came running over and kissed me on the mouth.

'Did you get my letter?' she asked.

'Yes.'

She threw her arms around my neck. 'Hold me,' she whispered. 'I feel so vulnerable after telling you those things.'

I held her in my arms and I could tell from the trembling in her body that she was telling the truth. I opened to her completely. We pulsed with love, our bodies flowering effortlessly, and at the same time a terrible apprehension rushing over me.

'What have we done?' I said. 'Falling in love is so dangerous.'

'That's why I got angry when you said that I only gambled with tokens and substitutes. First, because it used to be true and secondly because it isn't true any longer.' She looked at me with a shattering combination of trust and suspicion.

'This is so confusing,' she said. 'I opened up for the first time with you, even though I knew you were dying. It makes me feel mad, like I chose you because of that. Sometimes I wish we'd never met. It's a miracle to be able to feel again, but it's so raw. I have no detachment left, none at all. It's like a drug, it's so real. But I know I have to let go of you. If I stay with you it'll destroy me. If you leave now maybe I can thank you for bringing me back to life.'

I was transfixed by her emotions. I have never felt so close to another person.

'I can't stand you going,' she said, 'either now or ever, but I know I probably couldn't love you if you weren't. Christ, Charlie, it's so horrible. Can't you stop it from hurting?'

'Stay a little,' I mumbled, 'stay.'

Angelique brushed my cheeks with the back of her fingernails, her eyes brimming with tears.

'We need another day,' I said more forcefully. 'I'm not asking for any favours. I fetched the last of my money.'

'You have more money?'

'Yes, my last million francs. We can carry on just as before, but we'll have tomorrow to live consciously.'

'You expect so much from that word,' she said.

'Imagine the intensity,' I went on, 'now that we know everything. You see, I've reached a kind of barrier too. I was convinced that you were cold and manipulative. I was re-proaching myself for choosing someone who was bound to reject me. We've both been caught up in our histories, but tomorrow, for one day, we could set aside all the things that stop us from loving each other completely. And then we could part knowing at last what it means to be intimate with an-other person.'

'Yes,' she said, 'maximum intensity.'

I was moved when Angelique, who hadn't yet lost all the money I gave her at lunch, suggested we go home. We went straight to bed but, instead of the hectic passion we expected, found ourselves clinging to each other doubtfully. It wasn't that passion had been replaced by protectiveness; we were simply ap-palled by what was happening.

It was too late to hide and too late to reveal ourselves as well. We clung to each other, wishing we had never met; we rolled apart, wishing we could interfuse. Gradually the unease grew: the marrow fear, the worm on the hook, the tears in the womb, the screaming tedium of death's row, the unbearable thought of the unbearable thought. Angelique had told the truth. How brave, how distinguished, how futile. No shortage of ashes, not a phoenix in sight.

Neither of us slept all night.

'I can't stand this,' I said in the morning.

'You wanted another day,' she reminded me.

'Another forty years would suit me better,' I said.

'Another day like this,' she said, bent over her folded arms, as if she had been stabbed in the guts.

'I don't think I realized how frightened I am of dying until now,' I said. 'It's really desperate.'

'You're the one who wants to live *consciously*.' She spat out the word like a bad oyster.

'I think I thought it would be more rewarding.'

'There's nobody giving out prizes—'

'I'm not that stupid,' I interrupted. 'I just . . . when it comes down to it, I don't know where I got hold of the idea that it would be better to be in a more direct relationship with what's going on.'

'Neither do I,' she said. 'Nudist colonies are famously unsexy.'

'I almost forgot,' I said, walking over to the cupboard, fetching my small carrier bag and dropping it at her feet. I unzipped it and parted the flaps with my toe. She glanced down at the sheafs of fluorescent green banknotes. A desultory gleam, like a rat's tail, slithered across her expression and disappeared. I realized I had destroyed her way of life and I was offering her nothing to put in its place. She loves games because they have rules, their catastrophes are organized. By abandoning her gambling she set herself loose on a sea of unbounded emotion. 'The truth' wasn't just abstract and unconsoling, it had become positively malign, like being thrown an anchor after falling overboard.

The day hobbled on with unrelenting horror. By the time we got home again we were too tired to make love and too upset to sleep. We stared out of the window, admiring the suave transition from hideous day to hideous night.

Our parting was silent. There was nothing to say. Tears belonged to a luxurious world we had left far behind.

I went to the station and, contemplating the departures board, chose Toulon, the nearest place with no reputation for merriment.

17

I think continually of Angelique, the sharp crease of her thigh tendons, the soft hollow behind her knees, the throb of her jugular. I think of her on all fours, slippery with sweat, that last time when she turned her head and smiled, confident that I would enjoy myself, anxious that I would know she couldn't.

I want to lift her in my mouth like a lion cub and carry her to safety. I want to push my thumbs up her spine, vertebra by vertebra, until the pleasure floods her brain. I want to hook my arms around her shoulders and draw her closer. I imagine us foundering onto the bed, my chest against her back. We sink into a humming realm, a bell jar of bees, flesh buzzing. We are not absorbed in ourselves, or lost in each other, but both feeling the sting of the same rain, as if the rain was intelligence.

She begged me not to ring her after I left. It was easy enough to agree at the time, but the restorative influence of this terrifying loneliness has made me forget the agony of our parting and the seriousness of my promise. Perhaps she regrets her request and is longing for me to ring. I would do the kind thing if I had any idea what it was.

Impatience, when it intensifies beyond the banal agitation of the ticket queue, and the anguish of a pacing lover, changes its nature and nails one to the floor. Instead of a single stimulating obsession, a universe of cattle prods prevents the slightest movement. Today everything had the impossible urgency of already being too late. I spent the morning breathless on my hotel bed. If there was an Oscar for Best Corpse, I would currently be making the longest acceptance speech in the history of that sincere ceremony. Who could I not thank, what could I not thank, for bringing me to this perfect paralysis? A thousand lines of tumbling dominoes crash in on every moment, bringing their descent to the character of each situation. Of course the dominoes don't stop tumbling just because I call something a situation. The situation is itself a tumbling domino.

It is already too late to spend a significant amount of time with my daughter. Would it help her to be grasped by a dying stranger with the troubling title of 'Daddy'? I would do the kind thing if I had any idea what it was.

It is already too late to master the field of consciousness studies, a field which in any case trumpets the insoluble nature of its enquiry. You name it, it's already too late. I lay there, my thoughts anticipating themselves hopelessly and collapsing at their inception.

What finally got me off the bed was the wallpaper. I couldn't stand that fucking wallpaper.

Why can't I just crawl under a bush and die quietly? Why am I sitting here in the Brise Marine, waiting for the ferry to take me over to the island, worrying about how to put it, how to describe what happened to me this morning? The answer is simple. The moment I stop writing, a fungus invades my mind and, instead of the marble on which I was carving my epitaph, I am surrounded by the soft garbage of circumstance, my own death amounting to nothing more than a further mess.

Putting aside my reservations, I rang Heidi to arrange a time when I could see Ton Len. They were away for the weekend.

18

What an island! The straggling branches and peeling bark of the eucalyptuses in the dusty village square belong far further south than a short ferry ride. Outside the village, unmetalled roads turn into rocky paths. Shillings of light fall through the branches onto the wings of golden-tailed pheasants as they strut among the crunching leaves. Gulls lift from the sea spray and slice the salty sky. And the black sea, turned milky turquoise by the coast, heaves itself slowly onto the rocks and rushes down, pure white, in fleeting streams and cataracts. This is the southern coast, the wild side, looking out towards invisible land: Corsica, Sardinia, Africa.

Spring is too articulate to let winter ramble on. Vine shoots burst from its impatient mouth. Valleys that have never seen a bulldozer, thick with different greens – pine green, sage green, olive green, laurel green – are all tilted by the same wind and dazzled by the same sun.

I must bring my daughter here. However frightened I am of our love blossoming too late, I picture the two of us standing in this sickle bay, watching the clear ripples sift the black and gold sand at our feet. If we meet here, perhaps love will count for more than loss; perhaps she will always remember that I love her and hold the confidence in her heart.

I am not the person who was playing dead on a hotel bed yesterday, I am transfigured by beauty. I don't love these hills because they remind me of a woman's breasts, or love the sea because it recalls my piscean ancestry, or love this landscape because I've been taught to by Cézanne. The beauty is given, it is the order of things on which my suffering is imposed. Today I can see that clearly.

How do I know? Because if you jump out of a window, you can always tell when you've reached the ground.

19

Why do I bother with *On the Train*? If I have anything to say about the all-and-nothing subject of consciousness, why don't I just spit it out? Most things that can't be explained have the tact to remain unknown, whereas consciousness remains inexplicable despite being the only thing we know directly. One way of reformulating this mocking state of affairs is to say that the first-person perspective, which is the only witness to the quality of consciousness, cannot translate into the third-person perspective, the source of the scientific observations on which explanations are built. I had hoped to embody this frustration by writing a third-person narrative which is a flagrantly displaced first-person narrative. I also imagined that the tensions of these fictional conventions would create intriguing parallels with the tensions of the scientific method: the way the 'observer effect' and the participatory reality it entails conflict with the attempt to organize nature into laws; the way that the immutability of those laws conflicts with the claims of evolutionary theory. Ultimately, the way that science forms laws, by assuming that what has happened in the past will happen again in the future, means that science must by its own logic judge itself to be an inadequate description of reality, since it always has been in the past. There could have been a beautiful interplay between all of that and the notorious unreliabilities of narration.

Yes, if I had the time (and the intelligence), imagine the Fabergé bauble I might have wrought, nesting miniatures of itself, wrapped in a golden web of connections, at once floating and fundamental, compact and complete. It hovers before me, not unlike Macbeth's dagger, a reproach, a temptation, an illusion.

Still, there are things I can think about better by arranging them in a third-person narrative and so I'll plug on with my novella. Besides, I'm in a state of relative calm ideal for resuming *On the Train*. I've got hold of Heidi and she says that Ton Len will be coming down here next Friday with her nanny and a camera. For the last year I've had to try to set aside my frustrated paternal love so as not to go mad, but now it's fountaining irresistibly.

And yet as I sit here in front of this faded raspberry farmhouse, on a broken wicker chair, under the dusty eucalyptus tree, I feel the tingling of destiny, as if electrified sand has been poured through the crown of my head and is fizzing down through my body. I am grateful that my own mind is being ripped open again and again by dying and gambling and Angelique and my adorable daughter and the beauty of this island. The mess that's emerging, a confessional diary overwhelming the fragments of a speculative narrative, at least reflects the truth of my experience, the fact that every contemplation is interrupted, and that every interruption becomes a further object of contemplation, and that this rhythm of delusion and revelation feels as if it's essential to the nature of consciousness considering itself.

I keep thinking of my daughter's birth. The green accessories of the operating theatre, the friendly foreign nurses, the hard white light. Supine Heidi screened from her lower half by a tactful little curtain. The doctor performing the operation as crisply as a man tying his shoelaces. A Caesarean section could not distract him from planning a game of golf with his assistant. And then, with the flourish and the tenderness of a wine waiter, he eased the baby from her mother's womb and held her towards us, bloody, slimy, purple and open-eyed. I looked at her and saw that her eyes were full of knowledge and feeling. I had the intuitive certainty that she was already a person, without a vocabulary, a birth certificate or a wardrobe, but still a psychological unit whose development would take place in relation to something that was already present. What I loved so effortlessly was not something that was mine or something that was cute, but a person who was radiantly herself. It was not just her emotional intensity – she was furious to have the roof of her home cut open and to be dragged into the glare and pressure of a dry new world – but the person having the emotions who was present.

I realize that if I look into the implications of this intuition, it conflicts with my equally strong conviction that the self is a ludicrously contingent nonentity. Am I then locked into a debate between self and soul? These are not abstract questions, they are at the heart of finding out what the hell is going on. There isn't a human being on the planet who doesn't have a vocation for making sense; some people are just better at convincing themselves that they can.

Enough! This is just what I mean: these kinds of speculations are much better off in a third-person narrative where the self-contradictions can be reorganized as varying points of view within a lively debate.

20

There was nothing left to say about being stuck in Didcot and the rest of the conversation had come to a sympathetic halt. Crystal was swallowed by her preoccupations. Jean-Paul resumed his sense of the outer world as a conversation he couldn't help overhearing but had no desire to listen to. Patrick, driven by an old unease in the presence of social silence, scanned his memory of the conference for other points of entry into the subject that tormented them all.

The conference had taken him back to Oxford for the first time since he had been a student there. In those happily bygone days, he had found a city living under the spell of the high suicide rate for which it was celebrated throughout the world. Apart from the tramps who lined the crooked lanes and hideous shopping precincts with an air of belonging, everyone looked as if they were hurrying home to an overdose.

After rare and reluctant tutorials he would sprint back to the station feeling that a missed connection might turn into a life-threatening incident. It was generally as he passed Didcot that the possibility of enjoyment, excitement and lightness of spirit slowly returned to his terrorized mind. Perhaps he was still in the shadow of that habit; perhaps his mind would clear once the train broke free of that foggy junction.

Something about the set design of Oxford seemed to encourage posturing, to organize what were supposed to be unusually intelligent people into tribes of actors, as if no individuality could survive a fall into the deep trenches of tradition dug by all the oarsmen and dons and divinity students who had gone before. Eccentricity was the natural and in itself clichéd protest of slaughtered individuals.

On Patrick's first evening as a student, the warden of his college welcomed the new undergraduates with a speech. He praised the geographical position of Oxford. 'We're very well placed to go to London,' he said. And Heathrow, thought Patrick, dreaming as usual of New York. 'And Cambridge,' said the warden, 'which, of the newer universities, is, in my opinion, quite the best.' That's donnish humour, thought Patrick, deciding to take immediate advantage of London's proximity. The warden's sly, pedantic chuckle seemed to reverberate among the bookshops and gargoyles that guarded the taxi rank; his gurgling complacencies soaked the golden buildings until they split open like soggy trifle. Perhaps they had once been intended for something serious, but there had been too many puns, too many Latin tags, too many acrostics, too many fiendish crossword puzzles, too many witty misquota-

tions and too many sly chuckles for them to do anything but
rot, however noble and solid they might look to the winking
eye of a tourist's camera.

Returning to Oxford after ten years, he found that his
ear no longer picked up this paranoid frequency. He was a
sufficiently different person to return with some neutrality;
and, besides, he was no longer cultivating that narrative sense
of self which collects the resonances of earlier experiences.
The buildings seemed to have achieved that 'ordinary unhappiness' which Freud promised his star patients.

Patrick's attention drifted among the various incompat-
ible approaches to consciousness he had been exposed to over
the last three days. He hadn't yet organized his memories
of the conference into anecdote and he knew that unless he
gave them that structure they would slip down the nearest
drain. Once he had described what had happened, on the other
hand, the story would gradually colonize the experience, the
alternative details would disappear and only those that served
the story would be allowed to survive. The experience was already shaped by another story about who he was, but only the
feedback loop of description could give the experience enough
solidity to survive in active memory.

It was tempting to picture an ascending hierarchy of
complexity, with consciousness arising at the point where the
feedback loop occurred, but this just pushed the problem back,
leaving the loop unexplained.

The habit of asking 'why?' and 'how?' again and again
was like living with a four-year-old child. Patrick was exasperated by it and sometimes wanted to say, as he might at the

end of a long gauntlet of monotonous interrogation, 'Well, that's just how it is.' At other times, or sometimes at the same time, he felt that the measure of his strength was his ability to inhabit this vertigo of enquiry, to meet the eyeless gaze of the incomprehensible. Perhaps these two positions were not so different.

Patrick sighed and looked out of the unrevealing window. It was impossible for him to concentrate on the question of consciousness for long, impossible to turn away from it for any longer. At the conference, Galen Strawson had shown him Michael Frayn's parody of Wittgenstein about the man who doesn't know that there is fog on the road unless there is a sign saying 'fog'. 'This is the man who philosophers are always telling us about, the man who goes on asking for explanations when everything has been explained.' After going through some moves typical of a certain kind of analytic philosophy, this enquiring character asks, 'But how do I know that the expression "fog", where "fog" means "fog", means "fog", where "fog" means "fog"?' Someone suggests he is in a mental fog. 'Now one asks: "But how do you know it's a mental fog you're in?"' He, in turn, needs an illuminated sign saying 'mental fog'. The author concludes: 'If a lion could speak, it would not understand itself.'

If British Rail had been thoughtful enough to put a sign on the station platform, would it have said 'mental fog' or 'physical fog', and who would have been able to read it anyway? Perhaps in one of those fits of self-improvement which usually gave birth to a ticket with a name too complicated to request, they might have put 'metaphorical fog' or even, throwing caution to the winds, 'metaphysical fog'. What difference did it make?

Patrick could see Crystal reflected in the window. She seemed to have become inaccessible, and he felt his desire for her checked by the opaque surface which covered her disappearance. As to Jean-Paul, was it wise to interrupt him while he was reading a big shiny French book called *Le Mythe du sens*? Patrick was thrown wearily back onto his own thoughts. What kept him looking for clues in a sometimes infuriatingly abstract, technical and circular debate was the allergic relationship he had with so many of his own mental habits. He had to know whether there was anything free in the wretched drama of consciousness. What else was there in the end? A man's biography was the history of what he had given his attention to, and so it seemed worth knowing what attention was, and how it related to other types of knowledge.

'Oh, God,' muttered Patrick. He felt the constant longing to escape his own habits of expression, and then watched the tyranny of his taste, like a bullet in the heart of a skylark, reintroduce him to the inevitability of certain rhythms, certain symmetries, certain tricks of argument. Faced with this curvature of his imagination, he experienced a fresh outbreak of self-allergy. Maybe things hadn't changed that much since his student days.

All the agony about how consciousness related to the simultaneous firing of neurons seemed to Crystal relatively trivial. The correlations would become more compelling, there would be ever more bizarre brain lesions for the angel of empathy, Oliver Sacks, to describe. But even if the map came to match the territory in the spookiest possible way, there would still be a few hippies, philosophers and romantics who would insist that there was a real city under all that paper, a city of experience, lost in translation. The mapmakers would reply that there was indeed a city, the city described by Francis Crick where, 'You, your joys and sorrows, your memories and ambitions, your sense of personal identity and free will, are in fact no more than the behaviour of a vast assembly of nerve cells and their associated molecules.' Everybody would be back where they started but with more suggestive details. What was neuroscience worth in the consciousness debate when consciousness had its life in experience and she could never experience her neurons firing?

She was sometimes tempted to think that consciousness was the fundamental constant which physics had forgotten. The notion that the 'singularity' was a form of consciousness seemed rather less mystical, on balance, than the idea that the universe was born fifteen billion years ago out of nothing. Followed a few billions of years later by life, with consciousness arriving only just before the end of the party, struggling up the stairs against the downpour of entropy and species extinction, an afterthought resulting from activities in the central nervous system. 'A likely story,' as Peter was, or had been, fond of saying.

What appeared to be the tough existential decision to face up to our famous insignificance and isolation, a refusal to grab at the flimsy consolations of a purposeful cosmology, turned out to be a human monopoly of creative power. The universe, life and consciousness were allowed to lurch stupidly into existence, but for true creativity we must look to the Sistine Chapel, or the combustion engine. The Hubble telescope was a miracle for admiring an accident. No flies on the brave boys and girls, in white coats and black overcoats, who had banished superstition from their laboratories and cafes.

She was arguing, but who was she arguing with? Who were these people in white coats and black overcoats? As she recognized what she was doing, the argument began to fade. The thoughts were all hers. They settled back at their source. Her shoulders sank. She breathed out more slowly. She had retracted her attention from the contents of her thoughts – in this case a make-believe argument with a make-believe audience – and returned it to the subject, the thinker. But she was still observing herself, and thereby observing herself observe herself, in the infinite regress of the witness box. When the fixation on the object of thought had gone, there was still the witness observing its absence. Then there was no observer, just an experiencer. Then there was no experiencer, just experience. At last.

I have to stop writing my novel. I rang Heidi today and she told me that Ton Len will not be coming to see me after all. Someone called Dunan Rimpoche is doing a special healing ceremony, and Heidi has been told by her therapist that she ought to take Ton Len 'to heal the wound of her absent father'. She'll be in touch with me soon.

'When will that be?' I asked, trying to stay calm.

'I don't know. I don't like to set my plans in concrete.'

'I'm up to my mouth in concrete,' I said, 'and it's pouring in through every vent.'

'Oh, God, you're such a drama queen,' said Heidi. 'Anyhow, I'm not going to argue with you. I know how to set my boundaries these days and you can't make me feel guilty.'

'Why don't I come over and see you both tomorrow?'

'I don't think that would be very appropriate,' said Heidi.

Since then I've been lying on my bed. Through the warped windowpanes, the torn mosquito net and the half-closed shutters, I can see the corner of a plane tree, the seagulls drifting through a slit of sky, and some shivering bushes on the hillside, shining in the north wind, as if they had been splashed with cold water.

I could say that it is death that frightens me, but that would be too reassuring. It would give the impression that I know what is going on. Every day, it's true, I wake to the winning image of a revolver fired into my temple. It's true that my brains splash onto white tiles and my body slides down and slumps at the foot of a wall. I can't deny that it's upsetting, but why would my imagination go to so much trouble if suicide wasn't less upsetting than this limitless white terror, bleaching every object in its universe? I marvel at the optimism of suicide, expecting to bring torment to an end. Not to mention the executive elan, the rush of impatience that comes at the end of a long history of failed delegation – everybody employed to console you has let you down, and so you sigh and load the gun and say, 'It's always the same story: if you want something done properly, you have to do it yourself.'

The allure of suicide is to avoid the white terror and the al-

lure of everything else is to avoid suicide. Reactions react to reactions like worms impaling themselves more deeply on the
hooks they try to escape. If I refuse to elaborate this feeling,
maybe it will fold in on itself. An infinity of unease, given no
trade, might shut up shop and turn out to be as small and fleeting as happiness and love and vitality. Why should fear have any
more substance than the rest of them, unless I sustain its life with
evasion and credulity? Yes, I accept it all, the shame, the cirrhosis, the stupid and unkind things I've said, the boredom of this
fucking personality which has stopped me doing anything I don't
regret. The unacceptable has finally found its natural dumping
ground. Truckloads of hospital waste rain down on me and I
wait imperturbably for more. The white terror folds up like a
sheet, corner to corner, crease to crease. It can't stand being recognized for what it is: just another feeling. But what a feeling. I
think I'd better go for a walk.

21

It was late afternoon by the time I set out for my walk. Restless a few moments before, my limbs turned to coffins at the garden gate. If death is the end, terror. If it's not the end, terror too. Terror if nothing matters. Terror if it all matters absolutely. I haven't murdered anyone. I haven't raped anyone. I haven't stolen, or committed acts of arson. But I have had thoughts, and that's been more than enough.

I persevered and set off towards the southern coast. Everything was oppressively symbolic. I was chained to a rock having my liver eaten by vultures. If I had gone to the trouble of stealing fire from the gods, it might have seemed worthwhile. How could Heidi cocoon herself in frivolity and pettiness, while those sharp beaks tore at the last shreds of my life? It isn't achievement that makes our actions immortal, it's death. Whatever we've done when we die lasts for ever. If we've failed, we've failed for ever. There is so little time to pass on my love to my daughter, and when I die the catastrophe will be incorruptible. A spasm of loathing for Heidi suddenly animated my body and I stormed towards the Gorge du Loup, breathless with fury and panic. No human sounds distracted me from my state of mind, just the wind combing the pines and the sporadic clocking of the pheasants in the wood.

The path forked, both branches leading to the coast. I tried to gild my mood by taking the high road, but it turned out to curve towards the village. I doubled back and took the other path. The cheap symbol of the high road usurped by the cheap symbol of the wrong path. A lifetime of choosing the wrong path, I thought grandly.

I struggled to the clifftop, the sweat drying icily on my chest. The waves boomed in the Gorge du Loup. The wind was solid enough to support my leaning body and loud enough to make my screams inaudible. Although I was shouting, I couldn't quite make out what I was saying. I realized how little substance any of my feelings had without the loop of listening to myself think and speak. Better to stay on this clifftop having my thoughts ripped from me by a gale.

As the sun bled into the sea, the full moon surged out of the forest, stained red by the dying light. I fell silent, my mood shattered like the waves exploding on the coast below. Soon enough the colour drained from the moon and it turned back into sizzling white rock, making its arching progress over the island.

After this hammer blow of awe, I started to look suspiciously at what had happened. If terror was just another feeling, why was the sense of beauty any different? Wasn't it a 'quale' among 'qualia'? It was easy to prefer it to terror, but that didn't make it any more essential. From the point of view of consciousness, the fact that it derived from something out there in the world didn't alter the situation either. Consciousness was my total present awareness, whatever its content or the origin of its content.

I struggled to find something essential in the beauty itself, to give it some absolute independence. The moon rising opposite the setting sun, their perfect opposition turned into perfect intercourse, the sun and the moon mingling blood, the poignant clash of scales, an effect with a lifespan even shorter than mine, acted out on a celestial plane.

There were rules to these pleasures, I thought irritably, as I pounded down the silvery track to the Calanque de la Bréganconnet, where I intended to hide from the wind and the mesmeric curiosity of the lighthouse beam which had started to sweep the eastern end of the island. Under the wrapping paper of individual occasions there were always the same characteristics to aesthetic success, the stale surprises of conflict and reconciliation, variety and unity, symmetry and asymmetry. This and that were sometimes thrillingly supplemented by The Other. The Other was probably something Jean-Paul should think about. Not a bit of the other, but The Other, the French philosopher's d'Artagnan, always ready to leap from the rooftops and create a diversion. My thoughts were all over the place; even my own characters weren't safe.

The wind started to subside as I walked downhill. The *calanque* itself was almost still. I found a hollow in the rock and watched the frantic sea calmed and confused as it was funnelled towards the beach, sometimes crashing in, sometimes bobbing up indecisively. The moon was not yet shining into the creek, but I saw it whitening the waves further out to sea. Lines of seaweed were stranded on the sand, some dry, some lolling in the surf.

I seemed to have completely lost the conviction, which had come to me so triumphantly when I first arrived on the island, that beauty was the natural order of things. The first time I saw this coast I was blown away by its visual brilliance. Was I misled this evening by the lure of symbolic thinking? The sun and moon mingling blood – wasn't it enough that the moon was briefly reddened by the setting sun? And yet the idea that they were mingling blood had been the content of my thoughts at the time. The sexual, the tragic and the symbolic registers were as much part of my consciousness as the optical. Beauty could not depend on an allegedly direct encounter with the thing that seemed beautiful. No such directness was possible. The sun and the moon, even if I landed on them, would come to me in the form of knowledge. There could only be more or less intimacy with the mental reality in which they made their appearance. There might be a primordial encounter with that knowledge but not with the object itself. I was not being solipsistic. I didn't want to deny that the sun and the moon were out there, with a life-span of their own, somewhat longer than mine, and that some kinds of knowledge referred to the facts of the case whereas others did not. But whether it was Phoebus, skin cancer, a small yellow star, the bleeding sun or entropy that appeared in consciousness, real beauty could only come from this intimacy with mental reality, whatever it might contain, and not from the inherent beauty of the thing or the thought. Who has not noticed a mood swing turn the petal-coaxing sun into the maggot-breeding sun? Sometimes I am delighted by things being as they are, sometimes by their resemblance to something else. Sometimes understanding how things work weakens my desire for metaphor, sometimes the desire is sharpened by understanding how things work.

The moonlight had reached the creek by now and made it look like boiling mercury. Sandflies, celebrating a warm human presence, left the banks of seaweed and danced ecstatically on my body. As I sat in the hollow slapping my face and neck, the dichotomy between appearance and reality seemed to infold and disappear. One appearance was being replaced by another. Reality might be the sum of all possible appearances, some generated by science, some by art, some by psychosis; some known, some unknown, some unknowable. In that case it was forever out of reach. Or it might be an unbroken awareness of the content of consciousness, and of its nature, with one appearance being replaced by another: this was what I now meant by intimacy.

The oxymoronic violence I'd been subjected to since my fatal visit to the doctor had distracted me from pursuing this intimacy. At first, I glimpsed that my only chance of reconciling myself to the undistinguished heap of incidents which made up my life lay in that direction. But then I got caught up in Prozac and New York and gambling and Angelique and the mirage of love and money. Not to mention my scholarly efforts to understand the current consciousness debate, a debate which happens to contribute nothing to the resolution of the question.

I wondered again whether I should give up writing *On the Train*. It didn't seem likely to bring me any closer to my

objective. Maybe Patrick – who, strangely enough, also has cirrhosis – should carry the burden of some of the things that have
started to take shape for me on the beach. When writers imagine a character who is dying, or condemned to die, they all too
often make him ruminate about the past, worrying that he may
not have led a good life, or being haunted by some forking in the
road when he ran away from true love, or failed to save a friend's
life. Something with tons of flashbacks, and a big violin section. Either the character claims to have a few regrets but, then
again, too few to mention after page 300, or he has the incredible courage and honesty to regret everything and wish he had
not done it his way. In either case, the main feeling about dying,
namely that it's happening too soon, is blurred by a preoccupation with the past.

Well, those of us who are dying – as opposed to those who
are lounging around in their studies making dinner engage-
ments, and then reluctantly disconnecting the phone for twenty
minutes in order to browse through a medical textbook and look
up some realistic details – those of us who are really dying haven't
got time to ponder the past. The present is scintillating with
horror and precision. The past is a luxury for people who
think they have a future. Does my life have subtle connecting
threads, strange coincidences, uniting themes? You'd better
believe it. Things can't help repeating themselves, can't help
colliding. That's not meaning, it's where the search for meaning begins.

I was beginning to feel cold and hungry, and tempted to
return to the farmhouse, but I stayed crouched in the hollow,
feeling there was something I had overlooked. And then I real-

ized that beauty had seemed fundamental to me when I thought
I was going to see my daughter. Now that I was not going to see
her the conviction had deserted me. Sometimes the closest things
are the hardest to see. I was shattered by the stupidity of not noticing that my whole outlook pivoted on my daughter. That
feeling of panic and self-reproach when you realize, at exactly the
moment you slam the front door closed, that you've left the keys
inside, if it could be magnified a thousand times, would dimly
resemble the electrocuting shame that rushed through me on the
beach. Ton Len, I had forgotten Ton Len. When I saw her a year
ago, she was lying on the sofa and I held her small feet completely
in my hands and she smiled and looked at me with utter trust.
She knew I'd always be there to look after her. That's the picture
that comes back to me again and again. The smile, the trust. I
haven't written about it, but then again there's no mention of
camels in the Koran. Some things are too flagrant to point out
until they've shown a talent for hiding or getting lost. Last night
I doubled my betrayal by losing sight of her. I will almost certainly die too soon to see her again and I am powerless to do
anything about it.

And so I sat in the hollow, pinned down by the fascination
of the way that everybody hurts each other by trying to make
themselves happy. The pursuit of happiness is not so much an in-
alienable right as an inevitable disaster. I seemed to understand,
without needing to formulate it, how things had come to be as
they were, with my four-year-old daughter a thousand miles away,
the memory of her father's love drifting into the fog banks of
early childhood and infancy, her mother in a tangle of hatred and
spiritual ambition, and her hysterical and gloomy father fixed on

a strangely academic obsession. All the players without any re-
course to freedom. Locked.

I was stung by the irony of pursuing something I was calling intimacy, some relationship with mental reality which I
hadn't yet defined but was already invoking like a mantra, when
the ordinary intimacy of contact with the person I loved most
was absent from my life. I could sense a chain-mail landscape re-
ceding infinitely in every direction. Each generation linked by
steel. Everyone acting under the duress of circumstance and personality. What did it mean to be free in this situation? Did I
have to content myself with *amor fati*, the love of fate, doing will-
ingly what I must do anyway? Was that it? I noticed that I was
not breathing and started again hastily. I stopped slapping my
face and neck. My hands dropped to my side. If I wanted intimacy I could have it with the sandflies.

In the delirium of my longing to reassure Ton Len, I started
to think of the insects which were now eating my neck and hands
and face as the appetites of all the furious generations before
us, the troupe of hungry ghosts who had prepared the way for
this meticulous tangle of suffering. With every bite I imagined I
was offering them my blood, like a coin in a cup. Finally, when
my whole body was contorted with the desire to crush them, I
saw that my need for Ton Len to know that I loved her was itself
a hungry ghost. At that moment the ravenous troupe subsided,
appeased by blood and recognition. The emotions which had
seemed to be inextricably entangled with my love for Ton Len
– frustration, despair, longing, resentment, the desire to be a
good person – took on their own separate natures, leaving an un-
alloyed love radiating from my body through the rest of space.

I was jolted into a new clarity by this strange fantasy. I started to flick away the flies and scratch my bitten skin. I'm not interested in martyrdom, just in having as many lucid episodes as possible before the curtain drops.

The wind had died down and the glassy atmosphere it left behind was turning a lighter grey behind the high hill to the east of the creek. I sat very still for a moment as if I was made of glass as well. The icy moon had sunk out of view. I felt drained and light. I couldn't think any more, any more than I could have stopped thinking at the beginning of the night. My legs were half dead as I clambered to my feet. I tottered home like a dizzy pensioner.

22

I was welcomed back to the house by a pair of air-force fighters cracking the sky above my head, the sharp lines of their vapour trails turning to smears of lipstick against the lurid dawn. I can never sleep in daylight or, for that matter, in darkness, but at least at night I'm in with a chance. I knew I would have to bully my way through another day on the volatile fuel of coffee and desperation. After a bath, I dragged myself to the village and had breakfast at L'Escale. I've given Heidi the number of the cafe, in case she changes her mind. I can't help entertaining the superstition that my little breakthrough of the previous night, however buried it now is by exhaustion, will be rewarded by some transformation in her attitude. Just as I was mocking myself for this magical thinking, Jean-Baptiste, the barman, came over to tell me that a woman had telephoned last night and would call again in the afternoon. It must be Heidi. She is the only person who knows I'm here. I settled down for the day and, after my sixth double espresso, started to write as if there were no tomorrow.

After his period of silence and withdrawal, Jean-Paul felt lucid and calm and, if he was going to be impeccably honest, rather superior, among all these Anglo-Saxons who brought the atmosphere of Sherlock Holmes to intellectual life, observant only in its case-by-case myopia, and lacking that power of impertinent generalization to which it was so invigorating to return in a text such as *Le Mythe du sens*.

'Ladies and gentlemen, may we have your attention, please—'

The announcement broke off immediately.

Ah, no, thought Jean-Paul, not my attention, that is asking too much. Won't it be more than enough to leave part of my mind, as I inevitably do, receptive to the information of my senses, to let your dead words drift down and land on the ground of my awareness? You really can't expect me to leap up and catch those withered trophies.

Crystal didn't speculate: a man had been talking; now he wasn't.

What has secured our attention, thought Patrick, is the interruption of the message. More is said in the pauses, blah, blah, blah.

The announcement resumed. 'Due to circumstances beyond our control this train will be terminating at Didcot Junction. Coaches have been provided for passengers to continue their journey to London's Victoria coach station. The coaches are located outside the main entrance to the station. We apologize for any inconvenience.'

A collective, stoically English groan passed through the compartment.

'Circumstances beyond our control' is an excellent phrase, thought Patrick. There's hardly a statement that wouldn't be improved by mentioning them. 'Due to circumstances beyond my control it's my birthday today . . . Due to circumstances beyond our control we still don't know how consciousness works.'

By the time they arrived at the coach, there were too few seats for Jean-Paul, Crystal and Patrick to sit together. Crystal smiled forlornly at the others and sat down in the first free seat. Patrick walked down the aisle, hoping to find someone who would not awaken the monster of his intolerance. When he got to the back of the coach he settled there anyway.

Jean-Paul installed himself as near to Crystal as possible, a knight's move away as he saw it, two rows back, on the other side of the aisle. He knew that the man next to him was Derek Wood, the evolutionary psychologist, and he had no intention of talking to him. Jean-Paul took an aloof view of 'Evo-babble', as Crystal liked to call it. For him, what characterized the twentieth century, if one could put aside its dazzling achievements in the competing spheres of overpopulation and mass murder, was the way in which thoughts, behaviour and communication had been set adrift from the intentions of the person making them, first by psychoanalysis, leaving us helpless in the hidden face of the unconscious, and then by all the disciplines that could loosely be called structural. Evo-babble was the latest attempt to demonstrate the vast weight of prejudicial habit. It was, in Jean-Paul's estimation, a natural consequence of the famous death of God that his depressing omniscience should be redistributed among genetic, linguistic and cultural structures. Evo-babble trumpeted the maturity of facing up to the blindness of natural selection, without that blindness leading to any more freedom than the most rigid predestination.

'My wife's waiting for me at Paddington,' sighed Derek, ignoring Jean-Paul's hasty immersion in his book.

'You have been hunting in Oxford, and your wife is gathering you in Paddington,' said Jean-Paul drily.

'Oh dear,' said Derek, laughing too hard, 'I hope you're not making fun of evolutionary psychology. It's very easy to mock, very easy indeed.'

'There is no need to mock it,' said Jean-Paul. 'It is too banal to require mockery. If someone tells me that we spend more time standing on our feet than on our heads, mockery is an exaggerated response. We are clearly embedded in our bodies, in our ecologies, and in the history of our species. There is no doubt that the mind is modular and that its various modalities have evolved.'

'We see eye to eye, then,' said Derek.

'But if I am reading a page of Proust, let us say a scene from the final reception given by the Princesse de Guermantes in *Le Temps Retrouvé*, how will my appreciation of the complexity of this experience be enhanced by the knowledge that fifty thousand generations earlier the Prousts were wandering the plains of Africa, peeping greedily and apprehensively over the tall grass, without yet having attended even the most rudimentary cocktail party?'

'Oh, I think they would have attended a rudimentary cocktail party,' said Derek. 'You only have to watch a group of chimpanzees to know that. Language evolved from the pressures of social cooperation. Anyway, nobody could say that Proust was indifferent to the pecking order in his society, *and* it might be argued that he gave birth to so many books because he was unwilling to disseminate copies of his genes by the traditional method.'

'You are right,' said Jean-Paul, emphatically reopening his book. 'The more I think about it, the less I can tell the difference between Proust and a chimpanzee.'

'Oh, I think there's a very marked difference. For a start, I'm sure that Proust wasn't partial to PG Tips.' Derek chuckled. 'But the size of the difference is the very thing that makes one marvel at the power of natural selection.'

'And what about the experience of pure consciousness?' asked Jean-Paul, deciding to change his line of attack. 'Awareness of awareness – what would be the evolutionary utility of that?'

'If there *is* such a thing as pure consciousness – and I'm not much of a navel-gazer myself, so I won't enter into the semantics of it – ' said Derek with dismissive modesty, 'it doesn't require an evolutionary explanation. Consciousness had to exist before it could be moulded by natural selection, so, from that point of view, there is no task of explaining the *existence* of consciousness.'

'But if the various types, of consciousness – visual, cognitive, et cetera – evolved for their survival value, they are essen-
tially unlike awareness of awareness, which has no survival
content whatever.'

'Relaxation,' said Derek, 'there's tremendous survival
value in that. But, you know, in general, I like Chomsky's distinction between problems and mysteries, between scientific
questions which are amenable to a solution and those which
no imaginable set of experiments could resolve. It seems to
me that certain aspects of the attempt to create a science of
consciousness fall into the mystery category – free will, what
happens to consciousness after we die, that sort of thing.
What's nice from my perspective is that that makes complete
evolutionary sense. Our minds didn't evolve to solve those
problems, any more than our eyes evolved to see ultraviolet
light.'

Weary of being misunderstood, Jean-Paul was determined to bring the dialogue to an end. 'So, if I've understood
you correctly, evolutionary psychology has no need to explain
the existence of consciousness and no possibility of explaining what is interesting about it. Really, we were completely
lost before the invention of this discipline, huh?'

'Oh dear, you really aren't a fan,' said Derek. 'So, what's
your line of country?'

'Reading,' said Jean-Paul.

Crystal's eyes were closed. She definitely wasn't going to have
another conversation. Tiredness was good. There was nothing to feed her curiosity, nothing to distract her from her

anguish. She realized, with the thud of self-reproach reserved for the most blatant oversights and already accompanied by a shimmer of relief, that her whole journey to the conference was born of a desperate need for consolation. Her craving for answers to the questions posed so brutally by Peter's coma had partially disguised itself as a passion for science. Now she was left with the naked longing to be reassured.

But could she afford to seek consolation from a future where death was the only certainty? When he was asked about the origins of the universe, the existence of God, the mind–body problem, and his survival after death, the Buddha had remained silent. What had drawn her to the dharma in the first place was the fact that it was a practice and not a faith: something to do, not something to believe. She recalled the allegory of the wounded man who refuses to have a poisoned arrow removed until he knows the name of the man who wounded him, whether the arrow was curved or barbed, shot by a crossbow or a longbow: his inquisitive pedantry is the equivalent of refusing to seek liberation without knowing whether the soul is dependent on the body.

As she remembered these things, her relationship with the unknown seemed to reverse: instead of being paralysed by ignorance, she was liberated by agnosticism. Released from a sales conference of systems and models, she returned to the vivid and discreet life of her own mind. She realized that she doubted everything except the sense of freedom that came from acknowledging a world in which things were neither unreal nor endowed with an independent reality, but flowing into one another like the air flowing in and out of her lungs. With this return to simplicity came relief, as if she had thrown open the windows of a hospital room. She was no longer tired, and when she opened her eyes she saw that the coach was already passing through west London.

By the time they arrived at Victoria coach station, Patrick could hardly wait to tell Crystal the happy news that the problem of consciousness was insoluble. A man called McGinn, sitting next to him on the coach, had explained the whole thing with exemplary clarity. Instead of using the mystery of consciousness to unlock a world far stranger than the one we thought we were inhabiting, McGinn used it to lock us into our constitutional limitations: not only was the problem unsolved, it never could be solved. Something we did not know and could not know provided an entirely naturalistic explanation for the arising of consciousness from insensate matter. Patrick, who had been toying with a materialism in which our ignorance was not intrinsic to our faculties but confined to our understanding of matter, immediately saw the advantages of the more radically pessimistic 'cognitive closure', namely that it allowed him to stop thinking about the problem. Instead of wondering whether he would live long enough to see science crack the code, he could now legitimately turn his back on the entire question. His life had been spent trying to stop thinking about one thing or another – sex, drugs, cruelty, snobbery, money. Consciousness just happened to be today's relatively abstruse nightmare, the thing he couldn't get off his mind, and McGinn's analysis was the Betty Ford clinic he had been crying out for, a refuge for those who had been engaged in the compulsive futility of trying to find a common language with which to negotiate between the dictatorship of science and the anarchist guerrillas of introspection.

Why was the copula between the brain and the mind plunged in an obligatory darkness? He had to hang on to the argument while he shuffled down the crowded aisle of the coach, hang on for a few more minutes until he could explain it to Crystal. Then he would ask her to dinner and back to Ennismore Gardens for an in-depth seminar.

It would all be over soon. Whether he was a property dualist or a classical dualist, a mystic materialist or a silly old physicalist, whether he acknowledged that the mind was extended or he opted to be an out-and-out panpsychist: none of it mattered any more. No need to try to airlift causality to the seemingly calmer plane of functions or algorithms; no need to pretend that the mind which had produced computers suddenly turned out to be no more than the artefact it had wrought; no need to point out that the intelligence which appeared to belong to the computer was put there by the programmer not by the circuits; no need ever to mention Searle's Chinese Room Argument again. He felt like a debutante who, grimacing sceptically in the mirror, has tried on every dress in her wardrobe, and then, with a sudden all-over rush of authenticity, decided to stay at home with a plate of baked beans. His own plate of baked beans was the thought of how 'deplorably anthropocentric' it would be to imagine that our cognitive closure could be translated into any kind of objective eeriness. Why should reality be constrained by our conceptual powers? All was well with the world, it operated according to the laws of nature; it just so happened that the law which described the cause of our most intimate and inevitable experience was utterly and for ever incomprehensible. He could live with that. No problem.

Still, the point was not how it made him feel but what the argument was. That's what would provide the agenda for a midnight seminar. He was getting dangerously near the door. He could see Crystal going down the steps, followed hotly by the superfluous Jean-Paul. He must get the whole thing clear, like a diagram hanging in the translucent space of his imagination, the blueprint of a missile that would lay waste to the Great Consciousness Debate. On the one hand, the property of consciousness was not a perceptible property of the brain . . . Then there was the stuff about spatially defined properties . . . we're doomed to vacillate between the contingency and the necessity of the connection. On the other hand . . . Oh dear, he was already at the steps. Well, he could only hope the whole thing would come back to him once he started talking.

'It's very clear,' said Jean-Paul, pulling his suitcase out of the side of the coach, 'our primate minds were not designed to solve the problem of consciousness.'

'Well, quite,' said Patrick. 'On the one hand—'

'I've decided to limit myself to being tormented by what I know,' Crystal interrupted, 'and not take on the further torment of what I don't and probably can't know.'

'Forget the "probably",' said Patrick. 'The whole thing was explained to me . . .'

'We agree,' said Crystal. 'We agree in advance.'

'So we're all agreed that it's insoluble,' said Patrick doggedly. 'Perhaps we should celebrate over dinner.'

'I need some rest,' said Crystal, with a shivering smile. Seeing her weariness, Patrick was almost grateful to hear her refuse.

After an unconvincing exchange of phone numbers, the three characters dispersed into the damp London night, each locked in their partially private and, even to themselves, partially hidden minds, but all standing firmly on the common ground of having no explanation for the real nature of this tireless and fugitive mental display.

At this point, Jean-Baptiste fetched me to say that the call had come through. I hurried to the phone and said hello.

'Charlie! It's Arnie Cornfield. How are ya?'

'Arnie? I was told a woman was going to call,' I said stupidly.

'You only take calls from women now, you old rascal?' said Arnie. 'Taking it easy in the South of France, surrounded by beautiful women on some paradise island – not a bad lifestyle.'

'What's all this about, Arnie? Why are you calling me? Don't tell me you've found a package for *Smell the Flowers*?'

'I'm working on it.' Arnie giggled. 'Seriously, though, the reason I'm calling, apart from the pleasure of talking to you, which it always is, is that the Movie Channel wanna do an interview with you about *Aliens*. The bad news is that they need to know your medical status.'

'Well, when we met in New York four months ago, I had six months to live. You're good at figures, Arnie; work it out.'

'The decision is up to you . . .'

'Or, rather, it isn't up to me.'

'We're talking different "its". I'm talking television; you're talking terminal. I don't know any tactful way to put this, so I'm just going to put it out there. Either they can do an obituary piece, which would tie in very nicely with a retrospective: this was the man who gave you *The Frog Prince*, *Aliens with a Human Heart*, and so forth; or they could do a profile, and if your health should decline *totally* before it gets aired, a little note at the end, "Charlie Fairburn died *whenever*" – you know the type of thing; always a heartbreaker for the audience; makes it very real. They think, "My God, I loved that movie. I can't believe the guy who wrote that has actually passed away." '

'Tough decision,' I said, 'but I'm going to make it easy for you. They can do the obituary piece without the interview. And, Arnie, don't ever bother me with this bullshit again.'

'Doesn't sound like I'm going to have that many opportunities,' said Arnie. And then, feeling he might have bared his teeth a little too nakedly, 'I'm only trying to protect your interests,' he pleaded.

'Interest doesn't come in the plural any more. It's singular all the way to the end.'

'Never give up hope,' said Arnie, a million fatuously happy endings cluttering up his mind. '*Never*,' he repeated, his voice cracking with emotion, 'give up hope.'

'Why not?' I asked.

'They might discover a cure. Scientific breakthroughs are happening all the time; and, don't forget, when it comes to medicine, money talks.'

'That really would be a scientific breakthrough,' I said. 'I wonder what money would say if it could talk.' I launched into a dialogue. ' "I was in Joan Collins's wallet the other day." "Oh, were you? How is Joan? I don't know her personally but her lawyer once used me to leave a tip at the Ivy . . ." '

Arnie roared with laughter at my silly fantasy. 'Are you putting a patent on that concept?' he asked. 'Only, I have a writer – British guy called Ian – always looking for a concept, and I think *Money Talks* could be perfect for him. A couple of bills fall in love, get torn apart, reunited, solve a crime maybe, or find the autistic nine-year-old who's hacked into a secret government installation for brainwashing air-force pilots who *think* they've seen a UFO. Only the nine-year-old, and of course the audience, know that the head of the programme is actually *himself* an Alien, and that the entire human race is a crop for these Alien farmers – real sinister guys; they wear dungarees but they glow in the dark. That's what death is: the Alien harvest. And if the kid can crack the code, he can save the world and make us immortal . . . I'm just making this stuff up as I go along.'

'I can tell,' I said. 'Anyhow, the money talks concept is all yours, or Ian's.'

'Can I have that in writing?'

'Fuck off,' I said, hanging up the phone.

After the torpedo of Arnie's conversation, I sat dazed at my table. I watched the histrionic complaints being acted out at the bar, the islanders' inevitable insularity, railing against '*le continent*', the mock fights between men with drooping moustaches and smoker's coughs, a fisherman pretending to storm out and then winding his way back with an aria of insults, his hand chucking spadefuls of indignation over his shoulder, and I felt the violent alienation of those moments when everyone seems so trapped in their roles that they might as well not have an imagination, a dream life, a capacity for geometry – how long shall I make this list? I couldn't help wondering what roles I was caught up in myself. I might no longer be the alpha scriptwriter puttering around LA in his classic car, secretly delighted by the bad taste of his shirts, but wasn't I still dying in the shadow of some giant cliché? The *artiste maudit*, for instance, who says, if not out loud, 'My neglected children are scattered over the face of the earth, my body is in ruins, and my alimony payments are twenty times larger than my income, but just get a load of this paragraph about the umbrella pines.' Or the deathbed apologist who is persuaded by the creaking of vulture-laden branches to put away childish things and have a cassock sent round from the wardrobe department. The thought of being remembered for *Aliens with a Human Heart*, upsetting enough in itself, was especially bitter since I'd become a human with an alien heart. I couldn't have missed my true subject more completely.

I left the cafe and hurried out of the village like a hunted animal. Arnie had stolen my solitude and I had to shed the self he had conjured up before I could think again. The island was becoming too crowded and vulnerable. Calls could burst in from New York and flood me with strange preoccupations. 'Never give up hope.' That was Arnie's vision of my situation: an argument between hope and despair, probably resting on a still sillier struggle between optimism and pessimism. At least hope and despair were feelings; optimism and pessimism were emotional ideologies, or deals with fate. In the universal chiaroscuro, the Manichaean crevasses of daily life, it made no sense to latch on to one thing rather than another. There was no point in striving for anything but intimacy with mental reality.

I started to reinvoke the power of intimacy, but the feeling of insight which had accompanied the whispering of its name on the previous night was gone. What pressed in on me instead, as I walked along the dusty track to the Plage du Langoustier, was the impossibility of saying anything that was true, anything that didn't require qualification, anything that wasn't local and uncertain. I was obsessed by the trap that if knowledge is uncertain and causation inexorable, our sense of freedom rests on our ignorance. This thought is always available (I think Patrick had it at some point, or was it me?), but sometimes it insists on itself with a kind of leaden authority. The world again resolved itself into rippling lines of dominoes, falling through me, over me, past me, crashing down with every action I took and every thought I had.

I came to the top of the hill and looked down on the tapering south-western tip of the island, its bevel of beach, its wind-stooped bushes, and further out to sea, in a final rush of seclusion, a ruined tower crumbling on a rock of its own. I was suddenly gripped by the desire to swim out to the tower, to a place where Arnie couldn't telephone me, an ultra-island to which this island would be '*le continent*'. I walked down to the spit of land I had seen from the hill, intending to set out from the long, pale Plage du Langoustier, but seeing the sickle bay of Port Fay on the other side, and remembering that I had imagined taking Ton Len there and watching the clear ripples sift the black and gold sand at our feet, I decided instead to set out from there and swim to the tower round the end of the island. It was a much longer swim, but I'd stopped reflecting and was acting from impulses which were so rapid and imperious that they seemed to belong to a single trance.

The water was cold. By the time I reached the mouth of the bay I was shivering uncontrollably, but my mind was in a state of despairing calm, my gaze fixed on the grey crease of the horizon where the sea and sky seemed to meet, without in fact doing so. They just went rolling on in their parallel curvature, only brought together by storms, like the mind and the body forever separated by the 'explanatory gap' but brought together by the storm of life. The horizon was the home of delusion, pretending to reconcile the parallel curvature of the world. I must swim out there and denounce its lies. I was beyond the narcissistic impertinence of the lonely tower – '*Le Prince d'Aquitaine à la tour abolie*', the winding stair to the crumbling battlements – beyond all that. I was cold and tired, but I was furious as well, furious with all illusions of reconciliation. And what of intimacy? Was I going to let the vague potency of that word save my life? Was intimacy going to make me turn back and get dressed and stop this silliness and have a hot meal and get a good night's sleep? No. Intimacy was another blurred horizon, pretending to dissolve the observer and the observed, only to resurrect them the moment that the dissolution was recognized. I swam on with savage weariness.

As I finally broke free of the bay, I was confronted by a cream-coloured yacht. Ostentatiously old-fashioned, the inside of its funnels painted red, and several forests felled and varnished for its masts and saloons, it bore down on me with easy indifference.

Other people, I thought, other people were always ruining everything. Then again, what did it matter? I could just swim on. I would be out of sight by the time they could give me any unhelpful help. The yacht continued to bear down on me.

'Oy!' I shouted. 'Watch where you're going.'

It made no correction to its course. Its sharp bow was set to split the hemispheres of my convoluted brain. With a burst of speed I swam to the right. I had no intention of being exhibited at a consciousness conference as an unplanned example of one of Gazzaniga's split-brain patients. I needn't have bothered to move. The engines roared into reverse, and after the slithering indented clatter of the anchor chain the boat came to a halt, cut its engines and undulated serenely a few yards away.

The sudden expenditure of energy left my stately and thoughtful suicide in jeopardy. I also had to deal with the uncomfortable fact that I'd tried to save my life. Was I the mere plaything of animal instincts, the 'fuck, food, fight and flight' of evolutionary psychology? Or was I only prepared to kill myself on my own terms? Far from submitting to fate I was trying to exercise stylistic control over it; I was still playing a role.

'Coo-eeh!' someone called from the boat. I looked up, galvanized by an involuntary social habit. '*Excusez-moi, j'espère que vous nous*, I mean, *nous vous* . . . Charlie? Is that you? It's Pamela, Pamela Goodchild. What on earth are *you* doing here?'

'Drowning – until you came along.'

'Well, hop on board quickly! I'm sure Jean-Marc'll be delighted. It's his boat; isn't it lovely? Jean-Marc!' she called, looking over her shoulder. 'Guess who's off the starboard bow, if it is the starboard bow – I never know which is which.'

Jean-Marc appeared at the guard rail. 'Charlie! Your timing couldn't be more perfect. Marie-Louise was just complaining that we needed an extra man for lunch. Really, she has a genius for arranging these things.'

'John dropped out at the last moment,' said Pamela. 'I was *furious*. Whenever we have something really lovely planned, he wants to stay at home and doze off over some absolutely dire political memoirs.'

Silent with horror, I mounted the ladder as if it were a scaffold. The usual suspects littered the deck.

'What a small world,' said Pamela. 'It really is, isn't it?'

'In Spanish,' said Xavier, laughing like a hyena, 'we say "the world is a small handkerchief". *Maravilloso!* A small handkerchief.'

While these fools wittered on around me and a crew member rushed forward with a cream-coloured bathrobe, my eyes were drawn across the vast scrubbed deck to an unknown figure in a charcoal suit who stood with his back to us massaging a pair of shoulders in the chair below him. I knew with nauseating certainty that they belonged to Angelique.

'So, what were you doing on this charming island?' asked Jean-Marc.

'Taking the long swim,' I said.

He looked at me discerningly. 'Not, I hope, the "long swim" which Richard Burton threatens to take in *Night of the Iguana*?'

'Colder,' I said.

'My dear fellow,' he said, 'you must take a hot shower straight away.'

Angelique and her masseur remained perfectly self-absorbed

in their corner of the deck. I followed Jean-Marc through the sa-
loon and down some stairs into a rainforest mausoleum of mahogany and rosewood panels.

'I'll send one of the crew to fetch your clothes on shore,' he
said, leading me through the double doors of the master cabin.
'Or, if you prefer, you're welcome to borrow something...'

Stacks of cashmere sweaters, as tightly packed and finely
graded as a box of crayons, filled the teak cupboards of Jean-
Marc's virile wardrobe. Hanging opposite were rows of identical
off-white cotton trousers, pressed as crisply as folded paper,
and, above them, rows of identical softly corrugated corduroy
trousers. On brass rails at the foot of the cupboard was a tilted
display of tasselled loafers and blue canvas shoes.

'Great selection,' I said, wondering if I could slip through a
porthole and back into the freezing water. I thought of my three-
day-old clothes heaped on the beach, the balls of dirty socks
stuffed into the rotting shoes, and the huge coffee stain next to
the hole in my blue sweater, gone at the elbows. 'If you don't
mind, I'd love to ...'

'Anything you like,' said Jean-Marc, sliding open a few draw-
ers on his way out. 'We'll have lunch when you're ready, but
there's no hurry. It's really just a picnic.'

I washed the goose pimples from my skin under a steaming
shower and, feeling like the boy in *The Go-Between* who is bought
a green velvet suit by the rich family he spends the summer with,
returned to the deck wearing some of Jean-Marc's maddeningly
soft clothes. His South Sea Island cotton might as well have been
drenched in Nessus' blood.

The table was loaded with lobsters and glistening bowls of

mayonnaise and yellow-necked bottles of white wine, punctu-
ated by silver bread baskets and silver pepper mills. Everyone was
in the mood for a picnic.

'Ah, enfin,' said Marie-Louise. 'So, we can eat.' She angled
her cheeks expertly for the quickest kiss. 'I'm sure you remember Angelique,' she said confidently, 'but I don't think you've met
Dmitri.'

I nodded to the pointlessly good-looking man in the charcoal suit, and then said hello to Angelique, hoping to make her
share the alarming nostalgia which was flooding my body like
an injection. She answered me with cheerful shallowness. I could
tell that she was not just protecting herself, but already protected
enough by genuine unconcern.

I sank into my chair and listened to the cracking of lobster
shells, like distant gunfire. I felt closer to the lobsters than the
people who were eating them. Even the eggs which had gone into
the mayonnaise seemed to have been unfairly sacrificed. Why,
if it came to that, had the bright olive and the swelling grape
been crushed, if it was only to prolong the lives of these vile man-
nequins?

'Aren't you having one?' said Pamela, dragging a lobster tail
through a half-demolished hillock of mayonnaise. 'You're making a terrible mistake.'

'Have you noticed,' said Alessandro, 'that Jean-Marc's lobsters always taste better than anyone else's?'

'Hmm-mm,' everyone agreed, their mouths too full to form
a whole word.

'We must know your secret!' Alessandro demanded, his
swashbuckling finger dispatching all opposition.

'I think that Charlie needs a bowl of hot soup after his ordeal,' said Jean-Marc.

'The ordeal has only just begun,' I said.

'*Ah, non*,' said Jean-Marc, 'you're not going to swim back.
Nobody swims at this time of year; the water is an atrocious tem-
perature. *Jean-Pierre, amenez Monsieur une petite soupe bien
chaude*,' he instructed the swarthy butler who stood behind his
chair. 'Your timing couldn't be more perfect,' he went on. 'Lola
Richardson, who I know is an old friend of yours, is joining us
after lunch, and we're having a screening of *Flat*. I have a very,
very small projection room on board, but as long as it's you there's
room for one more.'

I suppose what I did next must have seemed odd to the
others, but the thought of seeing the Maestro's swan song in the
company of my self-appointed literary conscience was more than
I could bear. I couldn't plausibly claim to have urgent business,
and so I simply got up and walked back to the steps which led
down to the water. I peeled off Jean-Marc's luxurious clothes like
a man on fire.

'He seems to be the most *fanatical* swimmer,' said Pamela.

'He certainly has an extraordinary idea of good manners,'
said Marie-Louise.

'It's typi-cally English,' said Alessandro, delighted as
usual. 'So eccentric! Perhaps he is going to fetch more lobsters
for us.'

'More lobsters!' said Xavier, wheezing from the effort of
laughing so much.

I had left my swimming trunks to dry in the bathroom, and
so I was naked by the time the butler arrived with a bowl of soup.

I explained that my appetite had deserted me.

Just before I jumped into the shatteringly cold water, Angelique came up to the guard rail and whispered, 'You bastard, why didn't you call me?'

Back home I was dismembered by exhaustion and hunger. I made the bowl of soup I had refused on board *Les Enfants du Paradis*. The heat pulsed through my body in widening rings like the broadcast of an important victory. The scattered jigsaw puzzle of my attention reassembled into a single image. The sea and the sky didn't seem so far apart after all; 'the incense of the sea' drifts up and falls again in a gentle rain. I felt myself tumbling into sleep, but I knew already that it was time to leave. The beauty of the South of France has been embalmed on this little island. It can be visited like an inspiring tomb, helping people to imagine a time when the whole coast was wild, before land became property, and property became lots, and the lots became little. In the absence of nature and of land, there is natureland, a theme park of biodiversity, crammed with educational material and environmental projects, financed by a partnership between a regional council, a national park and an oil company. Infuriated by its lack of development, the air force roars overhead all day long, and the envious mainland disgorges boatloads of tourists hourly onto its fragile shores. Silence and darkness, which people used to be able to get by stepping outside their houses, are finished in Europe. There is always the hum of a road, the whine of a jet, the screech of a train, the glow of lights over the hill, and, in really remote areas, army exercises. I thought I might find some silence and darkness in Porquerolles, and although the lighthouse beam cornered me in the creek, there was a little silence, until the dawn patrol ripped open the sky.

It is time to go into a deeper solitude and find somewhere really empty for the final phase of my life.

23

The blue smoke of paraffin. The din of scooters. Narrow shops with stepladders to reach their high-rise stock, coarse sacks outside filled with grains and beans. The spattered colonnade, greasy smoke from the charcoal grills, little food stalls with vividly dirty shutters. The smell of the ground drenched in motor oil outside a mechanic's shop, wheels and fan belts dangling from the ceiling. Everywhere men hanging out. Some are slumped all day at a cafe table, sipping a bottle of Coca-Cola, stories of violence and passion blaring from the television. Some stare into space, their eyes emptied of all curiosity. They look perfectly prepared for death. I envy their sense of stylistic continuity. Staring blankly while their hearts beat, staring blankly when they stop beating. How agitated and self-concerned I seem by comparison. I must emulate their obedience. I am heading south until the will to live is baked out of me.

24

On the road, a mud wall enclosing a scrappy garden. Pointless gateways separating one expanse of broken stone from another. The increasingly beautiful absence of people. Big cloud shadows drifting across the brown plain, and then over a pinkish hill shot with a seam of darker rose. The eye meets no obstruction and the mind relaxes into infinity.

And then the dunes. We bounced and slithered over the sand. When we stopped, the flies moved in, feeding from the edge of my eyelids, cleaning their legs on my tear ducts, exploring my nostrils, tickling my lips, crawling deep into my ears as if they had something special to tell me. I came here for silence and I have put my head in a helmet of flies. There are no cars, no trains, no jets, none of those mechanical noises I was so anxious to escape, just the natural sound of a few hundred flies sampling my body and my food. Is it really such an improvement? Wouldn't

I prefer to have a high-speed train shooting through the end of my garden? Ibrahim wrapped a blue scarf around my face, leaving only my eyes exposed. I squeezed the arms of my dark glasses through the tight folds of the thin fabric, and still the flies crawled around the edge of the lenses, and searched every stitch of the scarf for a point of entry.

I set off among the small blonde dunes, tufted with grass, towards the darker orange of the bare dunes in the distance. The big dunes are voluptuous and dead: sharp tendons and hollow scoops and round mounds and sprawling limbs of pure sand. Closer, the few green blades among the pale dry grasses take on a brilliant intensity. Sand, tracks, dung, grass, flies, sky. There's a small pack to play with here in the desert. There aren't even palms and goat herds and oases and *bashi bazouks* and camel caravans and Bedouin encampments. Just sand, tracks, dung, grass, flies and sky. That's where I am and that's what there is here. And out of this poverty comes a necessary inwardness. All the distractions I have been running away from aren't here. I am falling without their resistance to lean on.

The far dune is far further than I thought. I run down the slopes, jog across the flat and labour up the far side of the sea of smaller dunes. The day is coming to a close by the time I reach the lower slopes of the big dune. I look back and after a search spot the white tents which Ibrahim and Mohammed have set up. I can't go back yet. I am fixated on the summit. The sun is going down and I'm worried about time. Worried about time – it's a miniature of my life. I make a contract with fate: if I can get to the top of the dune before the sun sets, I'll be healed. I don't stop to think what I mean by fate, or how it would reward me, or the countless superstitious deals which I've watched myself half-heartedly strike over the years. This is different: my whole being is unreflectingly locked into the contract.

To begin with, the route is hard and humped, but it soon narrows to a soft crease and from there a blade of sand curves up to the peak. With each step I have to excavate my foot and race to keep ahead of the sand which breaks away like snow in sheets and rivulets. It is as if I was running up the fugitive slopes of an hourglass. I have to stop and plant myself firmly while the sand rushes away around me, my heart beating violently. The wind grows stronger as I climb. The flies are fewer and then gone. They are hiding from the cold and the darkness that are rushing into the desert. I am heading away from any refuge, unsure of my footing, unsure of what will happen if I fall. The ridge is high and narrow. Will I bring tons of sand down on my unwilling somersaults? I imagine choking, my throat and lungs filling with sand. Now my lungs are the lower half of the hourglass. I untie the scarf around my neck. It seems to be strangling me.

There's no colour in the air except the white glare of the sun and the darkening blue of the sky. No clouds, no smoke, no dirt to catch and redden the light. This merciless clarity unmasks the sky and fills the atmosphere with the feeling of planetary solitude. It is beyond human emotions, in a colder, slower zone of mineral melancholy.

I make it up the last few yards to the peak and look out at the lower dunes. The rippling gold sinks into shadow. I wait for my reward. I'm in the Sahara, still gambling, still making deals. The sun slides down fast, leaving a white nimbus around the edges of the large dune opposite. There is no time to reflect. I have to hurry back to camp. In the desert, still keeping busy.

25

Moonless night, stars down to the ground. Clouds of breath streaming past my cheek. My feet swishing through the cold heavy sand. Walking to calm down. Stopping to calm down. Starting again to calm down. Everything is work, everything has to be earned. My watering eyes bring down a rain of needles from the feeble stars, stitching me into the night. How can I sleep in this silence, the blood hissing in my ears like a hostile crowd? I patrol twenty yards of frigid sand, working to exhaust myself.

I try the tent. Huggermugger in plastic dereliction. The floor covered in used handkerchiefs, empty bottles, dirty clothes, ripped packaging, a torch with a flickering yellow bulb. Outside, no limits; inside, no room. Then no limits inside, then none inside me. Agoraphobia on the bone, agoraphobia in the marrow. I struggle into my sleeping bag and, after half an hour of writhing, my arms pinned to my side and a cold zip in my mouth, imagine I'd be better off outside. And so I burst out of the tent like a swimmer coming up for air, and find myself back under the covered dish of stars, under the dazzling rain of diamond and sapphire needles, a prisoner of too much space.

26

Today a veil of sand is swaying unreliably over the ground. From the edge of this dune it pours into the air like an inverted waterfall. Sparkling and smoky, it snakes through the hollows, hissing against my boots. Most things change by falling apart, but the restlessness of the desert is a renovation. The landscape is priming its canvas again and again, like an amnesiac living on the shining cusp of oblivion. I can see the footsteps I made yesterday being blunted, buried and obliterated, and I feel the exhilaration of still being here to witness the brevity of the traces I've left behind.

A man in my position might easily head for the mountains and try to find consolation in their perseverance – never mind the rock slides, the sinking plateaux and erupting islands – or, at the opposite extreme, he might extort some pleasure from knowing that he will outlast the flies spinning on the windowsill, but neither of these strategies can match the sinister joy of watching the dunes replacing themselves with each other, as if the world could be destroyed and renewed by the same gesture, as if my sense of death could melt into a universe of change, like ice slipping from a tilted glass into a summer lake.

And then the wind died and the stars were at their steeliest. Morbidly swaddled in my sleeping bag, an electric shock of panic kept me from unconsciousness; I was like a sentry who stabs himself awake to avoid the capital crime of sleeping on his watch.

27

The next day I lay dozing in the tent all morning in a pool of sweat. I woke up fuddled and airless and dehydrated. After drinking a pint of warm water with a taste of baked plastic, I climbed a small dune and tried to clear my mind.

What struck me was the spontaneous transparency of consciousness. Consciousness and experience are synonymous. When I feel the sun warming my face I know it for what it is, nothing needs to be added. I don't have to tell myself a story: 'The sun is warming my face.' It is not a linguistic act. I don't have to observe myself to know the content of my consciousness, that is precisely what I know already. I may not understand my experience because I am confused, but then the experience I am having is confusion. Understanding may require analysis, knowledge requires facts, but this knowing is given. In its essence consciousness cannot be reduced to anything more fundamental.

Having no argument with my experience, there was no such thing as a non sequitur. I was just watching the pattern unfold, like a child playing cat's cradle with a piece of string. I was driven by local emotions into a freewheeling lateral association, or downwards in a potentially endless search for the anchor at the end of some chain of thought, or upwards into more and more denuded categories of categories.

And then, because this search can only find arbitrary resting places, it was the whole process, accepted with complete permissiveness, which became fundamental; its endlessness was its resting place: thoughts seemed to radiate from and collapse into the same source, as if the whole history of a star could be compressed into a single unimaginable image, a black hole as bright as the sun. This image disappeared into itself (because it was a thought within the process) and reappeared (because it was the image of the process in which it disappears) and there was no succession any more (because of its self-effacing appearance) and I was outside time (because there is no succession) and inside time (because I am a dying animal who has no reason to believe that he could have this experience without a living body).

And yet when I really accepted that I couldn't be outside time if I wasn't inside time, my whole being, and not just my identification with a particular aspect of my thoughts, was this speechless eloquence of still moving alpha omega part whole black light and I felt that I was participating in reality for once and not just hoping and moping, and all the oxymorons turned into paradoxes, all the watersheds into figures of eight, and I was as helpless as sand dancing on a beaten drum, but I was helpless from the strangeness of reality, not from some suburban despair induced by the insult of circumstance, and this helplessness was the greatest freedom I could know.

28

Six weeks have passed since I left the desert. My visionary moment curdled into loneliness and terror. I found myself cracking up, persecuted by all the little voices that were silenced by what I'd seen. Perhaps it's inevitable that the wave which flings itself highest up the beach should make the noisiest retreat. But what had I seen? Without the feeling of insight there was nothing left, nothing portable. I couldn't stay where I was, let alone go any further. All I wanted was to warm myself by the fake fire of reassurance. I didn't care if it was fake. I didn't want to think any more. I wanted to die in England. I wanted to see the crocuses in Hyde Park. I wanted to see my daughter one more time and hold her hand in mine.

Soon after arriving in London, I made an appointment with Dr Turner. I was hoping to get some painkillers that would catapult me into the only paradise for which there are any reliable

witnesses. Instead, he greeted me with the disturbing announcement of an experimental treatment for my condition. If I vol-
unteered for a trial at the King's Liver Unit I could start using it
straight away. Nobody knows the long-term effects, but the ini-
tial signs are promising. I felt my perfect despair prised open by
this oyster knife of good news. I had been so set on the certainty
of death that I couldn't separate my tentative relief from some
less obvious emotions. The luxury of knowing when I was going
to die, unknown to the athlete and the health-store freak, was
surprisingly hard to give up.

After leaving Turner's surgery I stood on the corner of Pont
Street, holding my breath so as not to absorb more than half the
cloud of diesel pumped into my face by an accelerating taxi, opposite the hotel where Oscar Wilde was arrested, and a few hundred yards from the prep school which first taught me to hate
education, searching for the secret glamour which is only vouch-
safed to the reprieved, but I did not find it in the stony face of
the jogger who hopped beside me at the zebra crossing, a mouse
squeak of rock music leaking from the headphones clamped to
his skull, or in the shimmering pelt which tottered across the
road with the wrong animal inside it, the quick and the wild
replaced by the contemptuous pallor of a powdered stick insect;
and I began to suspect that it was not gratitude for extra time,
but the incisiveness of approaching death which could cut
through to the heart of the matter, and I felt the bathos of survival, the loss of dramatic tension, the disappointment of watching the pristine violence of a mountain torrent thicken into a
bloated yellow serpent glittering its way slowly through the
crowded plain.

Now I would have to start again, writing silly screenplays, negotiating a mortgage, fighting with my ex-wife, struggling to secure a place in the world. I dragged myself across Cadogan Square, under the nervous buds of the plane trees, feeling the nausea of spring. No wonder Henry James, falling down after a stroke, thought he heard a voice saying, 'So, here it is at last, the Distinguished Thing.' He was expecting to be released from the triumphant mediocrity of life, its vulgar insistence on the inessential.

Today I finally called Heidi, my nerves sliding over sandpaper as I dialled her number. She took the news pretty well and after some hesitation suggested I pick up Ton Len from school this afternoon. We agreed on the details and signed off more tenderly than we have for years. After our conversation I felt such a tangle of excitement and weariness that it was impossible to do anything practical, and so I wandered into the street, killing time until Ton Len's school day ended. It was – is – one of those staccato spring days, sunburst and cloudshadow speeding overhead and underfoot, and in perfect harmony, simmering beatitude interlaced with the horror of watching the future wreathe itself around my attention.

I saw an advertisement for the Monet exhibition on the side of a bus and, with an impulsiveness I knew I would soon have to renounce, leapt on board and rode along Piccadilly to the Royal Academy. I hadn't realized that Monet had become as popular as a Cup Final, and I had to buy a triple-face-value ticket from an art-lover loitering by the gates.

I could hardly see the early canvases through the thrusting crowd, but when I reached the final room the scale of the *Grandes*

Decorations acted as a forcefield, holding the viewers at bay. I shuffled to the front and scanned the unframed lilac expanse of clouds hanging in water and waterlilies hanging in the sky. It drew me to its light-flooded centre only to diffuse me into the lilac pool, the pulse of ambiguity dilating into stillness. The water was a natural mirror for the mirror of art: once that dialogue of reflecting surfaces was set up, everything else – depth and surface, abstraction and representation, paint and painted – could enter into it, and when these compacted reflections reached their highest concentration there was a burst of freedom, the flashing moment when the eye perceives itself.

Monet said he wanted to paint the air, a task not unlike writing about consciousness, the medium for seeing which can't itself be seen. I have failed to paint the air or to write about consciousness, but it's enough to know that there are states of mind and works of art which deliver this paradox: that the thing which is closest to us is the most mysterious. Something I'd glimpsed in the desert was now in front of me, already made. The pleasure of recognition shimmered through my bloodstream. Obsessive reflection, which had sent my own mind falling and flailing over the last few months, stood before me like a serene piece of nature, and I felt like a walker on a cliff path who is met by a perfect gale and can lean effortlessly into the slope with outstretched arms.

I hurried out of the gallery, trying to protect this decaying impression. My attention was locked on to my imagination and I was almost run over as I crossed the street. Passing the window of Hatchard's bookshop, I saw the latest cluster of books to emerge from the great consciousness debate: *Emotional Intelligence,*

The Feeling Brain, The Heart's Reasons. I felt the giddy relief of knowing that I wasn't going to read any of them. The fact that science has decided to include emotion in its majestic world-view seems about as astute as an astronomer discovering the moon.

In five minutes I must go and fetch my daughter from her school. How will I tell her where I've been? My novel, thank goodness, is abandoned, and the sequel to *Aliens with a Human Heart* is unlikely to deliver any aesthetic charge, other than the stunned incredulity which sometimes sells fifty-three million tickets. Life is coming to get me, like the latest model of the sea monster in *Phèdre*, no longer the agent of divine cruelty but of pointless information, squelching down the beach, dragging its tail in the sea; it will soon crush me, downloading its scaly mass of triviality into my frail mind, but I am going to go down fighting, fighting for the flash of freedom at the heart of things.